Praise for Eric Barnes
and *The City Where We Once Lived*

"Barnes's new novel is a rare and truly original work: a hard-edged fable, tender and unflinching, in which a man's descent and renewal is mirrored by his city. An eerie, beautifully written, and profoundly humane book."

—Emily St. John Mandel, author of
National Book Award finalist *Station Eleven*

"A stunningly written tale of loss and grief. The stark beauty of Barnes's prose will pull you into a post-apocalyptic wasteland that is at once utterly foreign and hauntingly familiar. *The City Where We Once Lived* is a riveting journey through devastation, but one that delivers a world where seeds of hope emerge in the unlikeliest of places."

—Lindsay Moran, national bestselling author of *Blowing My Cover*

"Barnes has constructed an intricate apocalyptic world that frighteningly mirrors present-day reality."

—*Shelf Awareness*, starred review

"In bare-bones prose that is subtly affecting, the novel is a haunting portrait of why people form bonds and the many ways those bonds can be torn apart. . . . A story of adaption and the power of the human spirit."

—*Foreword*

"Exceptional . . . From the first pages all the way to the last, I was drawn in. I have read some dystopian future books in the past, but *The City Where We Once Lived* stands out among them."

—*Seattle Book Review*

"An all too realistic novel that could easily be ripped from future newspaper headlines, *The City Where We Once Lived* is a compelling read from first page to last and reveals author Eric Barnes to have a genuine flair for narrative driven storytelling. . . . Very highly recommended."

—*Midwest Book Review*

"Barnes's violent, haunted, and creepy novel about failing societies will attract readers of dark, postapocalyptic fiction."

—*Library Journal*

"Barnes has constructed an intricate apocalyptic world that frighteningly mirrors present-day reality. Through stark yet intimate prose, Barnes explores themes of separatism and displacement and how the lenses we look through are often distorted by lack of connection and empathy. He offers a cautionary tale about a world that feels a hair's-breadth away."

—*Malcolm Avenue Review*

"Taut with timely themes of climate change, waning empathy, and lack of community, the story hits scarily close to home."

—*Pop Culture Nerd*

"A highly recommended look at a dying city that is part dystopian and part premonition."

—*She Treads Softly*

"Written in a gorgeously spare language that perfectly reflects the dystopic future this novel depicts, *The City Where We Once Lived* kept me enthralled throughout. At the core is a deep and admirable compassion for humanity."

—Chris Offutt, author of *Country Dark*

"An intensely envisioned work of dystopian realism and American desolation, beautifully drawn from the slow-motion apocalypse of everyday life."

—Christopher Brown, author of *Tropic of Kansas*

"A most original novel, surprising and fierce—a dazzling puzzle of grief and utopia, dystopia, and hope."

—Minna Zallman Proctor, author of *Landslide*

"Spare and elegant, this novel brings into breathtaking relief a frighteningly recognizable future. Eric Barnes shows us what it means to inhabit—a building, a city, a life. And also what it means to be inhabited—by memories, by ghosts, and maybe, just maybe, by hope."

—Elise Blackwell, author of *The Lower Quarter* and *Hunger*

"A controlled burn of a book, full of horror and sadness and, once the fire dies down, the beauty of new growth. In the tradition of J. G. Ballard and Margaret Atwood, Eric Barnes gives us a dying neighborhood of outcasts who save the world that has cast them out. Just the book we need in these dystopian times."

—John Feffer, author of *Splinterlands*

"With deft prose and a discerning voice, *The City Where We Once Lived* is a taut examination of the archetypes and rituals that form the landscape of community."

—Courtney Miller Santo, author of *Three Story House*
and *The Roots of the Olive Tree*

"This novel stuck with me. The voice is appealingly quiet, the atmosphere dreamlike, but the premise of poisoned ground, weather gone haywire, and a government that has thrown up its hands, is frighteningly real. The most remarkable thing is that even after hope is gone, kindness survives."

—James Whorton, author of *Approximately Heaven* and *Angela Sloan*

ABOVE
THE ETHER

Also by Eric Barnes

Shimmer
Something Pretty, Something Beautiful
The City Where We Once Lived

ABOVE THE ETHER

A NOVEL

ERIC BARNES

Arcade Publishing • New York

First Edition

This is a work of fiction. Names, places, characters, and incidents are either the products of the author's imagination or are used fictitiously.

Arcade Publishing books may be purchased in bulk at special discounts for sales promotion, corporate gifts, fund-raising, or educational purposes. Special editions can also be created to specifications. For details, contact the Special Sales Department, Arcade Publishing, 307 West 36th Street, 11th Floor, New York, NY 10018 or arcade@skyhorsepublishing.com.

Arcade Publishing® is a registered trademark of Skyhorse Publishing, Inc.®, a Delaware corporation.

Visit our website at www.arcadepub.com.
Visit the author's site at ericbarnes.net.

10 9 8 7 6 5 4 3 2 1

Library of Congress Cataloging-in-Publication Data

Names: Barnes, Eric (Newspaper publisher), author.
Title: Above the ether: a novel / Eric Barnes.
Description: First edition. | New York: Arcade, [2019]
Identifiers: LCCN 2019004265 (print) | LCCN 2019008239 (ebook) | ISBN
    9781628729993 (ebook) | ISBN 9781628729986 (hardcover: alk. paper)
Subjects: | BISAC: FICTION / Science Fiction / Adventure. | FICTION /
    Literary. | GSAFD: Dystopias. | Science Fiction.
Classification: LCC PS3602.A8338 (ebook) | LCC PS3602.A8338 A63 2019 (print)
    | DDC 813/.6—dc23
LC record available at https://lccn.loc.gov/2019004265

Cover design by Erin Seaward-Hiatt
Cover photos: iStockphoto

Printed in the United States of America

For Reed and Mackenzie

And with more appreciation than can ever properly be expressed
for the music of A Silver Mt. Zion

ABOVE
THE ETHER

PROLOGUE

In some moments, the car will seem to fly. Floating, really, across the surface of the rainwater spread thick across the eight lanes of this highway, the cars around him so fast and the rain so heavy that he drives into white clouds formed from the ground, the mist and spray now rising up against the rain.

But still he drives faster.

His daughter speaks from the backseat. "Daddy," she asks, "where's Mom?"

The farmland is flat all around them, the water collecting in massive pools in the muddy and abandoned fields, so that the highway soaked with rain seems to fade into the landscape, the cars and trucks all speeding north, all the lanes, everyone heads north across the delta.

Nothing grows here, though. It's been that way for years.

On the radio, he hears the warnings.

But he doesn't want to look back.

His son speaks now. "Daddy?"

He moves the car left, into a gap between two trucks.

Keep moving. Keep moving faster.

He looks into the mirror. His daughter and son stare up at him. He shakes his head, saying, in a moment, "I still don't know."

• • •

In the bathroom, she pulls the sleeves of her blouse onto her arms, then puts her necklace around her throat. Watching herself in the hotel mirror.

She is beautiful.

Not as a girl she wasn't. Not as a teen. But, in her thirties, that changed.

He still sleeps in the bed. She can see him, behind her, in the mirror.

She isn't married. She has no children. She has never had a boyfriend. She thinks, if she thinks about it, that's how it will always be.

She begins to button the blouse, in the mirror now watching the sunrise in the tall windows behind her, floor to ceiling, a wall of windows that holds a sky turning pink behind the rows and rows of buildings. Fifty stories. Sixty.

This room is on floor seventy.

A minute later, she stands near the bed. Looking down at him. On the floor, she sees the money, hundred dollar bills, halfway out of the pocket of his jeans.

He's new to this.

She puts her suit jacket on. Sits down on the bed next to him, pulling back the sheets, and he wakes now, naked, looking at her.

She moves her hand along his thigh and across his belly, and she touches his chest, smooth, her fingers gliding along one of his nipples, then the other.

He stares. Thinking, probably, that she wants to start again.

Her hand touches the hair near his eyes. Feels it. Sliding the smooth, long strands between her thumb and finger.

Then she leaves.

She's in her office soon, a few blocks away, watching that same sunrise turn to daylight. Hot already, she can feel it, another day in the rising hundreds.

He was a young one, she thinks, for only a moment. Younger than he said he was. Younger than ever before.

• • •

The hillside just a mile away burns bright, the flames moving steadily toward a row of homes.

She watches from her front porch. The yard is massive. The house is too. A modern mansion, on a lot stretched across four acres of what was once forest.

2

The haze in the sky above their neighborhood colors the landscape in a permanent dusk.

The air smells like smoke. But she doesn't notice. The fires come so often that, now, what she'd notice is the absence of smoke. Clear air, that would wake her. Worry her. Confuse her senses and her mind.

Her husband watches her from the other side of the porch.

In truth, she died many years ago. To him. To herself. Her mind is frozen in the place where everything went wrong.

She'll stand watching the fires for hours. A glass of gin. Then another.

Eventually, he'll have gone to bed.

But still she watches the fires.

• • •

The two children in the backseat are quiet. Silenced by the spray of water rushing toward the car or by the speed of all the vehicles around them. Or, simply, they are quiet because of what they've left behind.

Home. Friends. Pets. Their rooms filled with the collected memories of childhood.

Cars wobble as they speed through the pools of water on the highway. A pickup truck nearby begins to veer, then spin, and it shoots off into the mud of former farmland along the highway.

It creates an opening and he quickly pushes the car into it. Moving faster.

This has gone on for half an hour.

• • •

Her office door is closed. She stands at her desk, the keyboard and three monitors elevated on steel arms, raised to meet her hands and eyes. Outside her door, she can barely hear the heavily muffled din of the company around her. People moving and conference calls and bullpens of young people joking into their phones, yelling at a coworker nearby, and laughing as they stare into their screens, as if their jobs are part of some sort of game.

She moves through numbers in the silence of her office.

Linking calculations, one embedded in another. Crossing companies and crossing countries and crossing financial instruments of all kinds. Building models of exceptional gains.

Her models always produce. Every one of them. Every time.

Heat presses against the windows, the glass stretching floor to ceiling. The windows are tinted, reflective, but if she touches the glass, she's sure her fingers might soon start to burn.

She doesn't once think about the boy.

• • •

Her sadness, her trauma, it constantly reoccurs. Every morning, sometimes every hour.

There is no release. Only moments of distraction.

She can see no fires near her home today. Just smoldering trees and the blackened shells of homes along the distant hillsides all around her. The trees and homes stand smoking among the curving roads built so unnaturally across this landscape, roads that once led people to their subdivisions filled with houses that were spread like a pox across these hillsides stripped of trees.

Mudslides in the winter. Fires in the spring.

"We could move," she hears her husband say.

"And do what with this house?" she says quickly.

"Leave it," he says. "Eventually, it's going to burn."

"We'll lose all our money," she says. "We'll go bankrupt."

It sounds to her like he's walking as he speaks. His voice shifting. Volume rising and falling with his movements. "Yes," she hears him say. "You're probably right."

"Then it's a stupid thing to have brought up," she says. "Or to even think."

He speaks after a while. "Okay."

"I can't imagine," she is saying, "why you'd bring that up."

He doesn't speak again. He may have gone inside.

"I can't imagine," she is saying, "why you'd think there's any way out of this."

. . .

His son asks from the backseat, "Have you checked the phone?"

"Yes," his father says, eyes forward, looking for gaps in the traffic. "I checked. There's still no signal."

"When did you check?"

"A few minutes ago."

He can see that the creeks and rivers they pass are rising too. Fed already by the swell of water from the Gulf behind them. Levees have broken, the radio says. Lakes have let loose their water. The massive river overflows, the radio says, the walls that held its course in place for decades have begun to crumble along many miles.

On the highway, the traffic has begun to slow slightly. The radio, the volume low, continues to warn about the danger behind them. The damage. And chaos.

His son leans forward from the backseat. Touches his father's shoulder.

"Check again."

. . .

Outside her wall of silent windows, the city seems to burn. Or to simply melt. The heat is obvious. Physical. A weight in the air.

In her office, she makes more money. Derivatives based on hundreds and thousands of other trades. She bets against some, and others she bets for, and all of them are linked together, here in her office, in the model on her computer.

It's very quiet here.

She sips from her water.

She opens her spreadsheet to another set of countries far away. Moving through scenarios. Methodically adding instruments to her plan.

But she'll go to the website soon. An order. An arrangement for later tonight.

. . .

"Homes should have never been built here," she says.

He nods.

"We should move," she says. "We should just leave."

He watches her. She's not looking at him. He says soon, "Okay. Let's move."

"Why didn't we move?" she says. "What were you thinking?"

He says in a moment, "I'm not sure."

"Always," she says, "always the same answer. *'I'm not sure.'*"

He says in a moment, "I'm sorry."

"And always," she says, "always you're sorry."

He says in a moment, "Okay."

She's standing at the window now. "Sorry," she says. *"Sorry."*

He checks the radio. Sets it to the emergency frequency. In case the fires start to come their way.

"Sorry," she says, *"sorry."*

He turns off the light in the kitchen. He heads upstairs to the room where he now sleeps.

"Sorry," she says, *"sorry."*

. . .

The cars on the highway flee water just three feet high. Not a wall. Were this the ocean, it'd be barely a wave. But it's the leading edge of a flood that will reach more than a hundred miles north and west. And it's no longer just water. It's a force of liquid earth, filled with objects from the ground and from homes and from buildings and from cars, the molten water turning in upon itself, branches and tires and animals and shingles, fed by rivers and lakes whose banks it destroys, pushing over everything it touches, pressing down on the earth, eating it alive, finding more water to help it grow stronger every mile.

The traffic has slowed. Almost stopped. The highway has narrowed down to two lanes. Cars use the medians, so still it's like there are four lanes going north. But the traffic is bumper-to-bumper. They barely crawl forward.

Without the motion of the cars, the rain no longer turns to clouds. Now, the water just falls, pelting the car, loudly, and the wipers can't possibly keep the windshield clear.

Without the focus on driving, his fear is rising. Through all his body.

The radio, volume low, explains how the water has come up creeks and rivers and it has crossed the flat, dead landscape, and it comes up the roads and it comes up the canals that were cut decades ago through the earth to ship cotton and beans from here down to the Gulf.

He sees a church, on a hill, the highest point he's seen since morning. One story, white wooden siding turned a greenish-gray with mold and decay.

The traffic has stopped moving.

On the radio, there's panic suppressed by the volume control. The near silent litany of a growing destruction. A city. More towns. The water is just three or four feet high. But that's all it takes to knock out whole stores. Whole factories. Whole blocks of homes and apartments and people.

The water is twenty miles behind them.

"The church," his daughter says. She's pointing toward the hill.

He looks at her in the mirror. He says soon, "We'll be okay."

"We should go up there," his son says.

"We'll be okay," the father says again.

"Daddy," his daughter says, "we hear the radio too."

PART I

ALL THAT THEY CAN SEE

They sit down, just the two of them, but not next to each other. Instead, they sit at a right angle on two big sofas in the lobby of a hotel, beneath an atrium of iron railings and yellow light that reaches nearly twenty stories above their heads.

They sit with a distance between them, automatically, a habit. But, already, he's begun to smile. As she talks. As he listens. Already he knows that he could listen, as she talks, all night.

CHAPTER I
THE FATHER

The dandelions grow everywhere.

Along cracks in the sidewalk and in the mortar of brick walls, and one after another the dandelions grow from gaps in the shingles on every house of every street for mile after mile. Buildings twenty and thirty and fifty stories high have roofs covered in young, green dandelions, dandelion stems growing from every windowsill, every terrace, every architectural outcropping otherwise unnoticed and forgotten.

There were signs the previous spring. Dandelions that couldn't be killed by any herbicide. Yet no one thought much of it. They were just an annoying number of dandelions in a lawn. Dandelions in the broken concrete of a driveway. Dandelions that homeowners and yardmen and work crews could easily pull free and toss away.

But now there are more than anyone can imagine. *Like cicadas,* people say. *Maybe some years are worse than others.*

The dandelions sprawl like cobwebs across whatever surface they've attached to, some are ten or twelve inches across, no flowers yet, no stem.

And still nothing will kill them. They can only be pulled from their place, carefully, with the roots intact, or else they will continue to spread across this city.

• • •

The car radio tells of the destruction to the south. Estimates of deaths are in the thousands. Maybe tens of thousands. Video, they say, shows the water simply pushing forward, in some places racing at twenty or thirty miles an hour. In other places, the water barely seems to move. Yet everywhere, its force continues to take down homes and buildings, turn trucks on their sides, push groups of cars from the surfaces of roads and the highway.

On another station, he hears baseball.

He's managed to edge the car to the side of the road. To a short dirt path leading up to the church.

He hears on yet another station that soon the water will lose its force. The wave, they say, will begin to slow. Any minute now.

Of course it will.

The small cemetery beside the church seems to be very slowly descending down the hill toward the farmland, a movement many decades in the making as the tombstones all began to tilt, eastward, and the stone plaques in the ground shifted, eastern edges lifting upward, western edges subsumed by the dirt and grass and moss.

There's a sign in front of the church. A message. Many letters are missing. But the scripture is still easily read.

HOW LONG WILL IT TAKE

FOR THE VISION TO BE FULFILLED?

—DANIEL 8:13

They've parked next to the cemetery, the kids sitting in the front seat next to him. Both of them pressed into the passenger seat, looking down at the rows of cars no longer moving on the highway at the foot of this hill.

They've been parked up here for just ten minutes.

His daughter holds the phone in her hand. She keeps hoping she'll get a signal.

"There are so many people calling each other," her brother says. "That's all it is. Just too many people trying to call."

He touches the boy's head. Then her head. Dark brown hand on their black hair. Warm.

They are seven and eight years old.

"Can either of you sleep?" the father asks. "You should sleep."

The boy, who's older, shakes his head. The girl does too.

"Okay," the father says softly. "Okay."

The wipers sweep water from the windshield. He's left the baseball game on the radio for now, the sound of a crowd simply talking and yelling and jeering at the batter, the announcer noting each step of each motion of the hitter and the pitcher and the runners on first and third.

Echoes of normalcy.

"Daddy," the boy says, pointing out the side window, south, where they've come from and where cars are lined up on the highway for as far as they can see.

The father finds the switch, pressing it, rolling the passenger window down to see better through the rain.

His son says, "People."

And he's right. Far away. Through the water in the air and the dimness of the sky and the blur of the near madness of a scene that's without context or reference for the father or his children, he sees what he thinks is at most an imagined nightmare, dark fears of the paranoid come suddenly true.

People, far away, are climbing onto the roofs of their cars.

Men and women and many children, all move forward, from roof top to roof top, even as the cars underneath them begin to shift, as if the earth below all of them were steadily giving way.

But really, it's the water. It pushes against vehicles, rocking them against each other, beginning to lift whole cars and whole trucks from the surface of the road.

And on the radio, the crowd cheers and cheers and cheers.

• • •

Still the dandelions grow.

In the grooves along the roofs of cars parked on city streets. In the benches of bus stop shelters lined with ads for joint relief and more efficient personal hygiene. Dandelions grow amid the flowers and shrubs of elaborately

14

contained landscaping in front of corporate headquarters, iconic steel towers, vast buildings made seemingly of one single sheet of glass.

The blades at the base of the dandelions grow tightly against whatever surface the roots have penetrated, the green blades jagged, rough, like weapons set out to defend against attack.

• • •

More cars lift, moving slowly but unnaturally, side to side and up and down, and some turn over, sluggishly, as if each were bubbling up against the heat of unseen flames somewhere underneath them. Solid rock turned methodically to red-hot molten lava.

But this is water. Pushing through and against the cars and trucks all stopped on the highway.

People climb from the cars ahead of the motion, running across rooftops and flatbeds and some jump down from the vehicles, trying to run between the cars or trying to run along any space on the shoulder of the highway still not covered by cars or trucks.

He watches. From the front seat. His kids next to him.

He thinks he should tell his children to look away.

Ahead of the water, some drivers turn their cars from the highway, trying to escape the gridlock by heading into the muddy land around them. The cars stop moving almost instantly, their front bumpers seeming to dive into the mud that the rain and approaching water have turned into a deep, thick trap that catches every car.

He thinks he should tell his children to turn their heads.

People stumble and fall as they run across the roofs. People carry children. People carry old men, they drag old women, one man holds a dog and a cat and some other animal unidentified, and now the man falls, forward, hitting his head as his body slams out of view. People jump from the roofs to the road and some try to run along the otherwise clear, seemingly safe path that the muddy, dead farmland seems to offer. But they stop moving immediately, sinking knee deep, their children sinking to their waists, caught within

15

a few steps by ground impossibly wet, all of them now only able to sway in place, swinging their arms, wildly geasping for help as the water from the south finally reaches them.

The father thinks he should tell his children to cover their eyes.

The water moves in a surge three or four feet high. Spread out across the farmland, pushing the cars and trucks from the relative height of the highway, a leveling force that keeps moving north. It rains still, hard, and so the only noise he and his children can hear in the car is the sound of the wipers on the windshield and the sound of the rain rattling hard on the metal roof of their car and somewhere, probably, they can hear the sound of their hearts, beating wildly, pounding, throbbing in their ears as the wave of water keeps pushing vehicles from the road and covering the people stuck in the land along the side of this dead highway, and the water sucks men and women from their windows and sometimes rises even higher, a swelling wave that pulls people from the roofs, because now the water has a force beyond its reach, a force gravitational that draws everything and everyone toward it.

He thinks he should grab them, his children, and hide them from all of this.

But he finds that he can't move. Can't blink.

He can't even speak.

• • •

In some places in the city, crews of two and three and four will move through an area—the landscaped plaza in front of an office building, the once ornate corner park near the art museum—and methodically remove the dandelions. Black garbage bags are filled. The men and women lean over, like day laborers in a field of produce, rapidly pulling dandelions from the crevices to which they've adhered.

In some places, it's obvious how many dandelions are missed. Left behind by a crew paid low wages for a job the landowners don't respect. Or missed because the dandelions have so easily found hidden places in which to grow.

Under rocks. Beneath other plants. In the dark recesses behind a bench.

Yet even when the dandelions have been pulled away with the greatest care, often some piece of root is left behind. Barely visible. But enough for that dandelion to, within a few days, easily regenerate, growing again, propagating once more across the surface of this city.

. . .

A few cars have managed to pull up this hillside to the church. Seven or eight of them. Other people run across the gravel road, then up the hill, tripping and sliding but still making their way forward. Away from the highway. Away from the water.

More people try to cross the farmland to the hillside. But these people skip the road, taking instead the straightest line from where they were to the promise of higher ground.

And now they are stuck. Thirty people trying to cross the farmland. The mud holds their legs. Their arms wave wildly, but without effect. The water soon surrounds them as they flail and, he's sure, all of them have started to scream.

He's gotten out of the car. To see better around him. The people who've made it to this hill are gathered in the small church cemetery. They stand on gravestones in the ground, or on tombstones that tipped over many decades ago, tombstones barely big enough to hold the feet of a man or woman. It's an overlook of sorts, the people all staring down at the chaos of the water and the endlessly flat land and the vehicles left in the spreading destruction.

Everyone stands on a tombstone. No one, it seems, wants to stand on the actual ground. As if this dirt too will soon turn into the mud that traps the people below.

Forty people on this hill. Maybe more. They watch.

But they hear nothing. The rain is just so loud.

The gravel road from this hill to the highway is gone now, the water pushed it away, and instead a river runs between their hill and the tops of destroyed vehicles along the highway, and there are fifty or sixty people up here now, in front of the church, looking back down at the water rushing and the cars being pushed left and right and turned onto their sides, and the people down there, those who try to swim, they are immediately overtaken by water filled with debris of a kind that won't allow kicking or arm movement; instead the swimmers are knocked unconscious or just pulled down, under, and already they are gone from view.

Other people, just a few, still stand on car roofs, balancing in place as their vehicle rocks and shakes and turns. Their arms are out. They are light on their feet. All of them are alone. Each one seeming to dance, bodies swaying to a song no one else could possibly hear.

• • •

And no matter how many dandelions are pulled up, there's a realization that this city was, some months ago, covered in tiny seeds that no one ever saw.

No warning went out. No alerts were raised.

Instead, without ever being noticed, some millions or billions of these seeds silently landed across the city.

• • •

Sooner than seems possible, the scene below the hillside begins to look as if it has always been this way. It is merely a lake, with a current moving slowly north, cut through with a ribbon-thin junkyard of cars and trucks, a bus, small vans.

Still people stand on the tombstones. Looking down.

The water hasn't risen further. It doesn't climb the hillside.

But it's impossible to say that anyone feels safe.

They simply know they are alive. They simply know they are, for now, protected.

The man is soaked. He starts to realize this. He feels cold first. Then feels water. Every part of him is wet. He thinks he should get back into his car. He turns to move, but his foot doesn't follow, stuck in the mud near the cemetery, and with his mouth open he emits a silent scream, a reaction so quick and so horrified that the motion of screaming is faster than his ability to make a sound, his hands now dropping to the ground, pulling on his calf, so hard that his foot comes out of his shoe.

His foot lifts easily. The shoe does too.

This is just mud.

Normal mud.

Nothing more.

He leans over. Head near his knees. Eyes closing tightly. Trying to breathe.

What in the hell do we do now?

In a minute, he stands up straight. Looking around. The rain falling, maybe harder than before. Near him, people still stand in the cemetery. But some also look around. At each other. At the church beside them.

Some move toward each other. Hugging. Touching hands.

Some move toward the church. The door is locked. But it's broken open very soon. Slowly, people move inside. Away from the rain. And from the highway down below them.

The father still stands next to his car. There is water as far as he can see, miles south and miles east and miles now to the north. Dark water, so heavy with mud that it has almost turned black, with a surface disturbed everywhere by branches and stray auto parts and the arm of a sofa and the leg of a chair and in too many places he can easily see the half sunken shape of a child.

There's no sense anyone can do anything to help the few people on the roofs of the remaining vehicles. They sit on the roofs. Or stand with legs stiff. One lies down, on her back, only staring up into the rain.

He gets back into his car. Turns the heat up. The kids stare at him.

"Daddy," his daughter says. "Have you checked the phone?"

. . .

The stems of the dandelions grow upward, six inches, ten inches; there are some nearly two feet tall. And then they bloom, one morning, in the heat of this city's constantly rising summer, the bright flowers color this massive and abused place in a brilliant, unmatchable yellow. Far more dandelions than had even been noticed, the blooms springing out from places impossibly high, impossibly hidden.

A city coated in blooms.

Days later, when the yellow flowers turn to white seeds, a billion perfectly round heads of fluff suddenly cover the city, the seeds releasing, and soon this place is enveloped in clouds of white dandelion seeds flying through the air. People wear surgical masks across their mouths, goggles over their eyes, they trudge slowly through the dandelion release, fighting their way forward as if a snowstorm has descended upon them.

The clouds blow lightly, down streets, over parks, against the tall clock tower and the huge art museum. The seeds stick everywhere, to people and to cars and to buses making their way up another crowded avenue, the buses' advertisements and logos and even the bus number and bus route all are obscured by the white layers of seeds.

And still more dandelions emerge. From places unseen.

Still more dandelions release their white and delicate clouds.

And already it's impossible to imagine how many more dandelions will follow these.

Traded banter and jokes they shouldn't share. All of it revealing slightly more than they know it should. Even as each line, each joke, each moment is hidden in teasing and in stories and in inappropriate comments too funny to be bad.

She lifts her foot toward him. "See?" she says, smiling, punch line to a joke only the two of them could decipher. "Shoes."

The atrium of the hotel, when either of them looks up into it, seems to bend, slightly, a house of mirrors maybe, ultimately vanishing upward, far beyond anything they can see.

CHAPTER 2

THE INVESTOR

The homeless teenagers sleep along Third Avenue, exactly one block from the nicest parts of downtown. Their bodies, lying asleep next to each other, inadvertently form an unofficial border that neither they nor the police will cross. An unspoken bargain with city leaders and law enforcement.

By day, though, the teenagers spread throughout the business district, some playing music for coins at busy street corners, others begging for food outside of packed restaurants, others just seeming to wander from alley to street or park.

A year ago, most rode the subways all day. Avoiding the heat. But then the city turned off the subway air conditioning. Budget cuts. And so now the homeless kids move across the surface of this city, finding shade in hidden doorways. Finding shade under massive overpasses. Finding shade in the shadows of ancient churches, under the overgrown trees and shrubs in city parks given over to illegal but allowed activities.

At night, though, they line up again. Along Third Avenue. On blankets or on sleeping bags. Some of them have only cardboard. Others have dogs, tan or black; the dogs lie quietly on the sidewalk, watching people approach. Many of the kids shoot heroin; others smoke pot. The line goes on for blocks and blocks.

All of the teenagers seem to be just fourteen. Maybe fifteen. Kids, really. Sleeping close to one another. Safety and community.

In this city, most all of them are white. In other cities, most all of them will be brown.

She grinds numbers in her mind, transaction on top of transaction, equations that circle in upon themselves as she closes her eyes, money multiplied,
money spawned, more money than she ever considered making. More than
she would want to spend. More money than she could ever possibly need.

"Tell me," she whispers, "about the first time you had sex."

She's moving forward as she says this, then back. On top of him. He's
inside her. But that's not enough.

She needs to hear his story.

"I was sixteen," he says, quietly, because she's asked him to be very quiet.
"She was older. She told me what to do."

She lifts off of him. Presses on his body with her hands, moving him.
Repositioning.

The light of this city at night is bright on the ceiling and walls of this
otherwise dim hotel room. Numbers still turn in her mind. Multiplying.
Connecting.

She has him in her mouth now.

"She undressed me," he says.

She lifts her mouth. "What were you wearing?"

"T-shirt," he says, breathing between each phrase. Quietly, though. She
likes that he can easily be so quiet. "And jeans."

"Buttons," she asks, lifting her head just slightly, "or a zipper?"

"Buttons," he whispers.

"In a bed?" she asks. "Or in a car?"

"In a bed," he whispers, pausing as she starts again. "My mother's bed.
She took off my jeans. My shirt. Slid my underwear down."

"Were you hard yet?" she asks.

"Yes," he whispers.

"Were you loud?" she asks.

"Yes," he whispers.

"Did you come fast?" she asks.

"Yes," he whispers.

23

She feels his hands touch her head. She lifts her own hands from his thighs, wraps her fingers around his wrists. She slowly presses his arms against the mattress. Lifts her own head to look at him.

"Don't do that," she says.

And then she starts on him again.

· · ·

In the cold cities, the homeless set up camps under bridges, or in the empty spaces between an overpass and an exit ramp, or on abandoned strips of asphalt, property owned by people or companies or trusts who've long since disappeared, whose connection to this place exists only in files stored deep in the basement of city hall.

The homeless build shelters to protect themselves from the cold. Tarps and cardboard boxes and stray pieces of unused plywood and pieces of corrugated metal from what were once backyard sheds. There are tiny worlds there, in the homeless camps. Leaders and followers and people with jobs to keep these communities alive. It's not all bad.

But it's a horror.

Both things can be true.

· · ·

Some she's seen before. The ones she enjoys. The ones who can be quiet. Who only talk when necessary. Who can answer her questions in a way that she finds satisfying.

It's all about what is satisfying.

"Did you come in her mouth?" she asks.

"Yes," he says.

"Did you come quickly?" she asks.

"Yes," he says.

"Did she swallow it?" she asks. "Or let it run from her mouth?

He's taking short breaths now. Quiet. Even shorter. "She let it run."

This goes on most nights.

She hates, more than anything, the television. It is loud and it is bright and the changes in volume and color happen much too quickly. She likes the quiet of her office. She likes the quiet of her apartment, after work, where she eats alone, before walking down the street to the hotel.

In the morning, she bets on oil. She bets on natural gas. She bets against a basket of new heart drugs after reading research that makes it obvious the drug will be only marginally effective. She bets on diabetes. She bets on joint replacements. She bets on gambling. She bets on gun sales, mood disorders, certain foods. She bets on water.

Her three analysts sit in chairs near her as she stands at her computer. All have the ability to speak quietly and quickly and only say things that should be spoken aloud.

She nods some, listening. The analysts lay out options.

She nods again. Listening.

On the screen, she folds in companies.

"Draw down everything from fund seven," she says. "Everything from fund nineteen."

They nod.

"Put it all into the Gulf," she says. "Oil. Gas. Nothing else."

The analysts all nod. One types, although silently, on a thin and silver laptop.

"Nothing else is worth betting on in the Gulf," she says. "Except the oil. Gas. That will all come back."

They nod.

"However," she says, and all three of them look up at her, "try to find a way to bet against any other type of recovery."

She turns in their direction. Looking now at the large, framed print behind them. A city aglow at night.

It's rare that she looks toward her analysts. She's only just realized this.

"Find every bet you can," she says, turning away again, reaching her hand toward her window, feeling the heat once more beginning to emanate through the glass, "find every possible bet against the recovery of whole towns and cities and populations of ruined and displaced people."

That so many of the homeless are mentally ill, ill by birth or by experience, is not a part of the discussion. Not for the people in the homeless camps. Not for the politicians who've chosen to leave them in their places.

That so many of the homeless are war wounded, limbs missing, faces deformed, or wounds to their guts or to their minds, all that is rarely part of the discussion either.

Person after person who live in the camps or sleep in the streets, so many doing drugs or giving over their bodies for cash or drugs or the simple right to fall asleep. Desperate, awful circumstances made normal by how common a scene they form.

In cities everywhere, the cafés and restaurants pay doormen to work the sidewalks: big men, some women, all burly and cold and hard, their role is to keep the homeless from pressing their faces against the windows.

• • •

"I would lie in bed," he whispers, "and all it took was to touch the pillow or a blanket or the mattress."

He's behind her, pushing. Not too fast. She likes this one. He learns quickly.

"So then I would start to rub," he says. "With my hand. On my under-pants."

She is flat against the mattress. Her head turned slightly, cheek resting on her forearm. Legs spread just enough. Feeling him move forward then back. Again and again. Listening.

"I didn't want to touch it with my bare hand, though," he says quietly. "So I would only rub against things. Press against a pillow. Against the mattress."

She breathes, deeply, eyes closed. Numbers spinning lightly in the very back of her mind. His hands don't touch her. They only press into the mattress near her arms.

"What else did you use?" she asks.

When she talks, she talks quietly. Over her shoulder. Whisper.

He hesitates, then says, "A stuffed alligator. That I won at the fair."

She breathes. "What else?"

It's a moment before he answers. "My cousin lived with us," he says, whispering now, even as he still pushes. "And I started stealing her panties. Pressing them against myself."

The numbers are evaporating. She can breathe deep. Listening. "Did you put them on?" she asks.

"Yes," he says.

"And her bras?"

"Yes," he says.

"Did you put her dresses on?" she asks.

He is breathing hard now, although quietly. And he's still moving slowly. Restraining. She likes that.

Restraint.

"Yes," he says.

"Did you look at yourself in the mirror?" she asks.

"Yes," he says.

"What color were the panties?" she asks.

"Pink," he whispers, "with tiny flowers. And the bra matched. And the dress," he whispers, voice breaking between each word—he wants very much to push harder and push faster, but he doesn't, he just whispers—"the dress was pink. But sheer. See-through."

Her mind is blank. She sees only him. In his cousin's room, panties and bra and dress, looking at himself in her full-length mirror.

"How did you feel?" she asks.

He breathes and rocks and pushes steadily into her. He whispers, "I felt pretty."

She turns her face, now pressing her chin against her arm. Rocking slightly forward with his motion. She says, "You can come now."

He is breathless, pressing, the same motion, restraining, pushing, as the air and motion and all of him is emptying, emptied.

Exactly as she wants.

And her mind, for now, stays blank.

• • •

Men and women push grocery carts, scavenging the city. They pull empty drink cans from the bins put out in front of homes and businesses, then crush the cans, pressing them down to their smallest form. Dropping them into black plastic bags tied to their loudly broken silver grocery carts. The bags steadily bloom outward throughout the day, a slow-motion expansion as each person finds more cans in the trash bags behind restaurants and in the overflowing and abandoned trash bins that dot the corners of downtown.

So many who are homeless.

Drink cans are the best find. They make many dollars every day.

• • •

She bets against grocery stores and utilities and local banks and insurance companies. She bets against city finances and bond issues and home mortgages and auto dealers.

She bets against them not just in the Gulf. But elsewhere. Wherever there might be a chance of trouble.

The heat, outside her window, she can touch it. Feel it grow.

Her office has a glass wall on the inside that looks out at the people trading. A hundred of them, at terminals and small desks. She worked among them for a time. Less than a year. She soon made the company and herself a sum her bosses could not quite comprehend. They asked her many questions. Checked into all her trades. Ran audits and launched inquiries.

All was clean.

Then her bosses offered her a team of twenty people. They offered her a bullpen on a floor only she and her team would occupy. They offered her dinners with rich investors and lunch meetings where she could lecture rooms of traders on what they were doing wrong.

She listened through all these offers. Nodding. "I want three analysts of my choosing," she said finally. "And an office with soundproof walls."

Sometimes during the day, she'll take a few minutes to watch through the glass wall of her office as the people on the trading floor move their lips.

"Tell me about the first time," she says now, in a hotel room.

The girl hesitates to answer. She's half dressed. Bra on, skirt. The woman has only just begun to undress her.

"A boy," she says. "My boyfriend. In his car."

The woman walks around her. Behind her. "How old were you?"

"Seventeen," she says.

"You're lying," the woman says, hands touching the girl's back, grazing the black bra straps, sliding her hands down to the girl's skirt. Unzipping.

"Yes," the girl says.

"Tell me," the woman whispers. She pulls lightly on the skirt. Lets it fall.

"Someone else," the girl says. "Older."

The woman is standing behind her, hands moving slowly down the girl's sides, across her belly.

The girl says quietly, "He was always nice to me."

"Of course," the woman says. "Of course."

"He was like family," the girl says, whispering.

"How old?" the woman asks.

In a moment, the girl says, "I was fifteen."

The woman unclips the girl's bra, slides the straps from her shoulders, lets it fall to the floor, touching the girl's nipples now, then sliding one hand down her belly again.

"I finally went to his house at night," the girl says. "Snuck out my window. He lived nearby."

The woman runs her fingers along the top edge of the girl's panties. Slowly. Back and forth. "And what happened?"

"He finally asked if he could hug me."

"Of course, he did," the woman says.

The girl is crying quietly.

"What did you wear?" the woman asks, hand in the girl's panties now, fingers touching. Wet.

"Sunday dress. Yellow."

"And underneath?"

"A lacy bra," she says. "He'd given it to me. And satin panties. He gave those too."

"And you got into his bed," the woman whispers. Her face is near the girl's eyes. Wet.

"Yes," she says.

"Was he gentle?" the woman asks, fingers gliding slowly.

"Yes," she says.

"Did it hurt?" the woman asks.

"Yes," she says.

The woman kisses the girl's neck lightly. Then kisses it again. Her hand is still in her panties. Working slowly. Steadily.

"And you went back," the woman says.

"Yes," the girl says.

"Again and again," the woman says.

"Yes," she says, crying harder now, breathing deeply.

"Of course you did."

The girl rocks forward, back. Just barely.

"And he came inside you," the woman says.

"Yes," the girl says, breathing harder, crying harder.

"Every time," the woman says. "Inside you. That's all he ever wanted."

She is nodding. Breathing harder.

"To come inside you. Again and again and again."

• • •

The emergency rooms hire security guards to rid them of their problems with the homeless. The scabies-ridden and the flu-infected and the panicked who fear their chest pains are a heart attack.

They are sent away. Driven off. There's no place for them in these hospitals.

Very few are welcome here. Only those who are nearly dead. Or are well-insured. Only the women giving birth. Or the people whose hearts have, after much abuse, finally stopped their beating.

• • •

She hates the television. In all and every form. She hates movies, and she hates websites that have video or ads in motion or anything but the written word. She only reads. Newspapers and magazines, and she reads books about string theory and biogeography and black holes and the role of famine and coal and salt in the development of civilization.

In print or on a screen.

As long as the screen is clean of anything but the simple typescript of written words.

She reads all this over dinner, at her apartment. Cooking for herself. Snapper with olive oil and red peppers, sautéed in a sauce with wine. Basmati rice cooked with sea salt and fresh pine nuts. Yellow squash grilled lightly with pepper and asiago. She cooks this for herself. Eating and reading, and it takes an hour or two before she'll send a message to a maid who'll enter the apartment to clean up what she's cooked.

But before she's interrupted by the person who cleans and after she's spent her time in the motion of cooking herself dinner, that's when she can be alone in the silence of her apartment atop this building. Views of the city and the port on the bay, lit up to a kind of daylight, the containers colored red and orange and yellow and green, in motion, transported, from ship to crane to truck or train, and beyond the port, she can see the airplanes taking off, jets ascending or descending; she likes it when they land, nearing the ground, ready to alight on the crowded outskirts of this overgrown and searing city.

She stares sometimes, out the window. For thirty minutes at a time.

• • •

31

Old women position themselves on the most populated street corners. They bring their own dirty paper cups. They pull their shawls up over their heads, motioning for their young offspring to sit down on plastic buckets or old tires or cardboard boxes spread on the ground. Everyone puts a hand out. Asking for change.

Help me. You must help.

Later in the day, the old women and their children will be picked up. By a husband or an uncle or a brother driving a dented, worn-out van. Their scam works eight to five.

And afterward, they return to their shacks underneath the bridge.

She is vulnerable. That's part of it.

She wonders what he's thinking. What he's feeling. What he might want or think of her.

And in his mind, he thinks the same about her. It's no different.

She is vulnerable.

It's an opening. To finally be himself.

CHAPTER 3
THE STRANGER

The animals, in some places, congregate in wild and enormous packs.

The water, in some places, has become entirely undrinkable. Or so scarce nothing can live.

The trees and shrubs and flowers in so many places have begun to suddenly turn brown, fading as they die.

• • •

It is snowing now, from a sky that has no clouds. The snow doesn't stick. But it snows this way some days, heavy flakes that fill the air, conjured by a madman trying to trick the world into believing the impossible is real.

She stands in her yard, letting the snow touch her face, feeling it evaporate almost immediately, thin, barely visible wisps of steam now rising from her cheeks, then crossing past her eyes.

This happens for a few minutes. Sometimes it goes on for many hours. Once it went on all day.

Then the fires on the hillsides nearby will start again. And the sky will turn dark, and the horizon will be heavy with thickly orange and brown and awful smoke, and she'll be left to watch as homes in the near distance erupt in flames that the fire trucks don't even attempt to stop.

"Come inside," her husband says.

She ignores him.

He says it again, and again she's ignoring him, "Please come inside."

She knows, though, that if he didn't ask, that would make her angry.

Their oldest child died. The other ran away. It's been two years since this happened.

Pictures of children on their walls that seem to her like the glossy, perfect photos supplied in the picture frames when she first bought them in a store. She doesn't recognize the faces. She has only her memories. Mental images of her children when they were very young.

The oldest son died at sixteen. The youngest son ran away the following year, when he reached sixteen too.

Her husband is a surgeon. She is a corporate lawyer. This wasn't supposed to happen. Nothing like this. Not at all.

She knows, of course, that she herself is sick. As a result of what has happened.

But she won't admit it.

To admit it would only make the pain pour out. But this way, now, it's contained.

Her oldest son's illness grew and grew. Depression, manic outbursts, steady self-abuse. Finally, an overdose. She fought to stop each step.

But in the end the mental illness simply passed to everyone else inside their home. Her. Her husband. Then her youngest son.

Sometimes, she can't blame her boy for running away.

Many days during the midst of it, the worst of it, she woke up tired, with her eyes tight from a night of crying and her throat raw from a night of screaming, and all she would want to do is finally run away.

• • •

Water laden with lead and chlorine and huge quantities of benzene.

Water that runs brown throughout the summer, emitting the smell of plastic or oil or rot.

Water that can't be found in remotely sufficient quantities.

People in some cities can't cook with their water or bathe with it or wash their clothes or clean their dishes in a way that they are confident their kids are safe.

Bottled water must be shipped from hundreds of miles away.

Reservoirs hit critical levels earlier and earlier in the season.

Farmland for hundreds of miles is no longer cost-effective to be planted.

Vast ranches where the irrigation ditches long ago went dry and the deep wells were drained completely. Ranches that are eventually abandoned. The livestock slaughtered. What's left of the land soon occupied by angry survivalists barricading themselves away from the worst they're sure will come.

And the communities farther upstream, all of which supplied irrigation for so long, they have all determined it is best to keep the remaining flow for themselves.

• • •

She wakes and realizes that she needs to drive to the coast.

She drives through fog in early morning light, seeing the outline of the sun through the heavy mist behind her. She sees bare, black trees emerge then disappear in front of her. The highway bends slowly, almost beautifully. Left, then right. Over a rise, then down. Cars disappear from her view, as if sinking into some abyss.

The fog gets thick. Dissipates. It gets thick again.

She feels for a moment as if she doesn't move, that it's the sun that moves behind her, the trees that hurtle toward her. But, of course, they don't. It is nearly silent here, in the car, the fog seeming to absorb the noise her vehicle surely makes, so quiet that she can hear her breath only as it escapes her mouth.

Sunlight breaks through the fog, then the fog takes the light away.

A world stripped down to just four tones. White and gray. Black and brown.

It will take two hours to get to the ocean. She follows a route that avoids all cities. Because she hates all cities. Her entire life. The filth and the crowds. The homeless people everywhere. Crime at every turn. Break-ins, rapes, and murder.

She needed to raise her children in the safety of a suburb. The safety of a new community carefully fenced off from the rising danger. The protection

36

of a security system on their doors and walls and windows, a guard who patrolled their subdivision, and the safety of new schools built on vast, stripped-down tracts of land. The knowledge they were surrounded by people of endless means, well-educated, every possibility arrayed before them.

And all of it far from everything going wrong in the city an hour from their home.

The highway bends, she enters fog, thick; she can see only thirty or forty feet in front of her.

Something went wrong with her oldest son. She can't identify it. When it started. Why. Her son turned on her, slowly, hints of anger, a deeper disdain. Just teenage stuff, she thought. Until it turned to near violence. Angry at others. Angry at himself. He was suddenly always angry. And most of all, angry at his mother. Angry that she made him angry. Angry that she tried to help. Angry that she said a word. Angry when she said nothing.

The fog is thicker, a heavy mist that lets her see just her hood, thin glimpses of the road, none of the brown forests around here. She drives, though, forward, feeling the highway turn. Feeling the highway sink.

The therapists tell her it's as if he had a hole so deep and painful. A hole he couldn't possibly bear or live with or control. And so he had to fill it. With anger, with alcohol, with driving cars a hundred miles an hour down narrow, suburban roads. But those things filled the hole for only a very limited time. So then he needed to find a reason for it. Find a reason for the sourceless, endless pain.

That's when he decides, they said, *that the source is you.*

The fog breaks, suddenly, the sunlight so bright behind her, lighting up the ocean, blue, the coast, a beach.

Mothers bear the worst of it, they said. *No matter what they do. We have no answer why,* they said. *It is simply a great unfairness.*

But even blaming her wasn't enough. Her son's anger wasn't enough. Drinking, speeding, fighting with strangers and students at school. None of it was enough. And so he turned to stronger drugs. They're everywhere, she learned. He bought them at the grocery store. At a dance. In the classroom. On a playground. And so, he just kept using them. Trying to fill that hole.

She parks the car along the side of the road, tires in the sand. She walks down to the beach. Forty steps, fifty. Waves are crashing toward her. The air smells thick, low tide, like the seaweed and foam and driftwood all across the beach have been left here just to rot.

Mothers are targeted. By their troubled, sinking children.

She knows that now.

Mothers bear the worst of it.

In almost every circumstance.

Fathers are only crushed. Abandoned. Left vacant and destroyed.

For mothers, it's much worse.

She reaches down. Touches water.

Cold.

There was a hole, bottomless, that he had to fill.

Even in the wind, the morning air is so hot that it's hard to breathe.

She turns around. Walks back to her car. And begins her long drive home.

• • •

Dogs move in packs through sprawling neighborhoods of poorly built, identical homes. Seven and eight dogs at a time, rising at night, when the heat relents, and they roam in search of food, in search of mates, knocking over trash cans, killing feral cats by the dozen. The packs of dogs inevitably run into other packs, much growling, some barking, all of them circling warily. If there's food in play, or a bitch in heat, the circling soon turns violent, clouds of dust rising as dogs scream and dogs bite and dogs tear into the flesh of one another.

You can hear it, from windows half a mile away. The frenzied desperation of wild animals in the street, all simply trying to live another day.

• • •

She rises in the evening in her hot and sun-dried neighborhood. A sprawling, hillside subdivision cooked to brown and red. Too hot to sleep. No electricity at night. The power will turn on at some point in the morning, in advance

38

of the highest heat of the day to come. A daily allocation of what power can be generated.

It's a region slowly turning its clock upside down. More people working at night in order to sleep during the day. Schools convene at three in the afternoon, sports played only in the late evening of the weekends, under lights paid for entirely by donations from the wealthy.

Power is limited. Brownouts are common.

And as people move away from the failing services and the fires that consume so many homes, the problems just get worse. Fewer people to pay for the many needs that now remain.

But she doesn't care.

She wakes at night and goes to her porch. Drinking gin. Looking up toward the subdivisions on the nearby hills. No flames tonight. Just the smoke from fires from a week or more ago, still lingering in the air above her.

"Can't sleep?" her husband asks. He's on the porch, in a chair.

She doesn't answer. Of course, she cannot sleep. Neither can he. *Why would we talk about this?*

Gin touches her teeth. As she exhales, she feels its vapor escape her nose. She drinks again.

Their neighbor runs his generator. His house is a hundred yards away. But she hears it running. The wife had a baby. She saw an email somewhere.

"We should bring a gift to the woman next door," she says.

"I did," her husband says. "Last week. We talked about it."

She turns to him. Staring. "I'm sorry. I forgot that. But I'll be sure never to forget such a thing again. Actually, I won't forget anything. Nothing. Ever again. But if I do, if I manage to forget one thing, you be sure to tell me. Right? Make sure you point that out. As quickly as you can. So that I apologize. And repent. Okay? That's what I should do. Repent."

He looks away. There's a moon through the red sky, turning a burning orange amid the haze.

"Or is it," she says now, armed with a new breath, "that there's no point in my apologizing? Right? It's a sin. Like all my failings. They are sins. And all of them unforgivable."

He stands. "I think I'll walk."

"I've reacted badly," she says. "Right? Again. Always the overreaction."

He moves down the steps, into the yard, walking carefully away as he soon disappears into the dark.

But she only stares at that moon. Breathing gin through her open mouth. Burning fire through her blurring eyes. Shooting flames in all directions from her mind.

Her house is filled with ghosts. The ghosts of children who once lived here.

But ghosts aren't just born of the dead, she's realized. Or the absent. Or the missing. The living can be ghosts as well. Her sons became ghosts even as they still occupied this house. Fragmentary beings, mere shadows of what they'd been, they moved like ghosts through her home's wide halls.

Her husband, too, became a ghost eventually. He once yelled. He once screamed. He once stormed through the house, in a voice so angry it was physical.

But now he sits.

On the other side of the room.

The other side of the porch.

Saying little.

Watching.

Watching her.

In no way trying to reach her.

He's a ghost too.

Just like she is.

She knows all this. He does too.

They've been this way for years.

• • •

In other cities, cats roam everywhere. Along streets and on the roofs of stores, and they emerge four and five at a time from sewer drains and broken vents leading into tall, abandoned buildings. Some are feral cats, generations in the wild; their coats and teeth and eyes speak to years and years of self-survival.

The cats eat whatever scraps they find in the alleys behind stores and restaurants. They swarm garbage cans put out on trash day. They swarm trees to kill the nesting birds. They descend frantically into sewers and under homes, feasting on rats and mice and even roaches, the tiny rodent bones and the empty shells of the large insects strewn along gutters and in alleys and in the backyards of homes in every neighborhood.

In the evenings, the cats cry out, howling to one another.

In the mornings, the sunrise is free of the sound of birds.

He has forgotten, as always, the ways in which she's pretty.

He's never forgotten that she's pretty. He couldn't.

He's tried.

But he forgets the many ways.

Her eyes. The way she holds a glass. The way she sits near him on this sofa.

Falling in love with her is many years in the making.

CHAPTER 4
THE FATHER

People on small and cheap computers connecting instantly across oceans once insurmountable. Camera phones better than the telescopes that first studied the stars. Games so totally immersive, so thoroughly intoxicating, that people pay to watch them played.

Meeting women, meeting men, seeking children, seeking sex.

Faces lit blue and white, in the windows of buildings across the cities, window after window, smiling and crying and so many of them carry an expression somehow suspended, waiting, hours they'll wait, as they stare into their screens.

• • •

Days later, the water has receded. Slowly returning to the Gulf, to the rivers and lakes from which it had escaped, but also it lingers in newly formed bodies of water. Lakes where there'd been lifeless farms. Creeks where there'd been streets.

The surface of the highway and the farmland around their hill has become visible again. But the ground between the hill and the asphalt is still soaked with water.

Mud so heavy and deep that it's obvious it will envelop anyone who tries to cross it.

The smell of chemicals and rot, carried here by that water and mud.

The rain has weakened. An intermittent drizzle from a sky low and gray and uniform except for the darkly swirling clouds that float underneath the

43

gray. The dark clouds move rapidly, racing across the flattened landscape, pouring impossible amounts of water until the clouds finally drain themselves.

His kids sleep in the backseat.

It's morning, early. He's slept a few hours in the front seat.

Two different helicopters have flown past them in recent days. One of them was military. It didn't vary from its course. The other was from a TV station, and it circled for a few minutes as everyone on the hill waved their hands and arms. Disaster footage. Captured. Ten seconds of video to give color to a discussion of the scale of the destruction.

But at least people know they're here.

In his mind, he catalogs their remaining food. Enough for four more days. *We'll be fine,* he says to himself. There's plenty of water, collected in a plastic container he made from a large bottle that he sets out on the hood of the car.

In his mind, he pictures fleeing their apartment, putting food into a duffel bag. They'd grabbed items in a barely controlled, nearly frantic state. "Get your sleeping bags," he ordered his kids. "Get your blankets. Grab clothes. Grab one stuffed animal."

The kids had been screaming at first, crying and panicked, and so he took thirty seconds, thirty precious seconds, to kneel down. Hold them both. Calm them. "I'm not mad," he said quietly. "Don't be scared. I'm not mad. It's just my work voice. Okay? Just a work voice. But we have to go. Listen. Don't be scared. But listen to every word I say."

He grabbed more blankets. He grabbed the tool box. Grabbed two kitchen knives. Grabbed flashlights. Grabbed batteries. Grabbed a bag of kids' books. Grabbed his computer. Grabbed his phone.

He had no shovel. No axe. All the outdoor tools were in storage.

He had no matches. No means to create a fire.

But don't panic. Just focus. Grab what you need. Get the kids in the car. Get the kids in the car and flee.

They'd felt the earthquake in their apartment. But there was also the hurricane centered south of them. Over the Gulf. And so, as the earthquake ended, he had a sudden thought. Fear, but something rational. The hurricane was massive. The biggest yet. And even though the worst of it was bypassing the city, the storm was also pressing down on the Gulf at highest tide. Levees and flood controls far to the south had already been breached by the storm.

And now an earthquake. In the Gulf.

He'd seen news reports of past tsunamis in other countries.

Can that happen here?

"To the car," he told the kids. "Quickly. Stay in front of me. We're walking fast. Don't run. We're walking fast."

That he had a full tank of gas was just dumb luck. That the new apartment was near the highway was just dumb luck. That it was Sunday, afternoon, minimal traffic, that was dumb luck too.

As he got onto the highway, he saw a few cars like his, packed up, frantically prepared, running from what they feared would come.

Once more he catalogs the food that's left in the car.

He's shared much of their food with the others on the hill. Other people have shared food too. For him, though, he's only done so because he didn't want his children to see otherwise. Had he been able to save all the food for his children, he thinks he wouldn't have shared it. Not in order to save himself. But to save his children.

That's all he's thought about for days. *How do I save my children?*

Outside the car, people are emerging from the church. Men, a woman alone, sometimes couples. They walk out onto the small porch, then into the yard. Some go to the cemetery, once more standing on the tombstones leaning forward in the grass.

The people look around. There's not much else to do. Assessing another morning on this lone hillside in the delta.

The group is not particularly friendly with one another. There's no anger. No fighting. But there's no sense of community or camaraderie either.

It's more tolerance. A wary willingness to aid but not sacrifice.

They are wounded, after all. Each one of them. Scared and scarred by what they saw, what they did, by what almost happened to all of them.

Clearly, no one has much ability to help anyone but themselves.

· · ·

The crash of cars is broadcast real time, unfiltered and unedited.

The debates of city councils are aired real time, long-winded, rambling, dull.

The sex fetishes of old men are shown real time, women set up on small beds, willing to do anything for a range of progressively higher fees.

· · ·

On the radio, he hears about the oil leaks in the Gulf. Twenty oil rigs. Maybe more. All damaged, some completely overturned, sinking or already sunk. Oil slicks, at least twenty of them, growing every day.

He hears the speculation on the numbers dead. Tens of thousands. Much of the city and the suburbs were hit with the wave of water. Whole buildings taken down. Entire neighborhoods swept flat and clean. People trapped in their cars as they tried to drive away. The water beating many to death with the simple force of its arrival.

There are, though, tens of thousands of people who survived by making it to one of the elevated highways in the city. Others made it by staying in tall buildings, buildings strong enough to have survived the force of the rushing water.

As it traveled north up the delta, the water gained strength via its destruction. It broke through levees holding back massive man-made lakes. It broke through levees holding the river in place for most of the last century.

These lakes, the river and its tributaries, their positions and courses had seemed permanent, forever fixed. But now all were suddenly released. Because in fact those locations were only precariously maintained, water held against its will, now finally set free.

The water joined the wave from the Gulf. And on it kept pushing forward.

It's warm outside now. The clouds have broken. The sun shines steadily. And by the end of the day, the landscape is soon coated not in mud but dust.

"How long will we stay here?" his son asks.

The three of them sit on the hood of the car.

"I'm not sure," the father says. "We can't get across the mud yet. All that mud at the bottom of the hill." He turns to them. "But it will dry. Maybe a few more days. And we'll be able to leave."

On the highway, over the past few hours, they've begun to see vehicles moving slowly north. Not vehicles that survived the flood on the highway. None did. But these cars somehow survived what happened to the south. High ground. Now they slowly make their way through the wrecked and meandering maze.

His daughter holds the phone. She is looking down at it. Staring. It's every few minutes that she blinks.

The kids have stopped asking if the phone works. Instead, they just reach for it periodically. A smooth black object, made of glass and metal and plastic, they turn it over and over in their small hands.

He did have one text from her. Days ago.

In the moments after the earthquake. When the sirens started and the radio and TV announced what had happened in the Gulf. When some people, like him, guessed what might come next.

He saw a message on the phone. From her. But he didn't tell the kids. There was no way they should read it.

Take them. Now. And go. Because I can't imagine I will survive.

• • •

Maps accurate to the square foot, guiding you to what you're trying to find.

Don't worry, don't look around.

Just listen. To the voice. Telling you what you need to do.

• • •

The phone is ringing. It's dark. The middle of the night. It takes him a few rings to wake up. To realize what the sound is.

"Did you get out?" she asks, desperately. "Where are you?"

"Yes," he says. "About a hundred miles to the north. Then the water reached us. But we made it up a hill. By a church. We've been stuck here since then. But the kids are fine. They're completely fine."

He can hear her crying.

In a moment, he asks, "Where are you?"

It's a long moment before she responds. He thinks he's lost connection. "Downtown," she says. "The condo. The building survived. Ones nearby did not."

He says in a moment, "Good. Okay. That's good."

He turns to the kids, in the backseat. His son is opening his eyes. "Wake up," he says quietly. "Both of you. Wake up. It's Mom."

As he hands the phone to them, the kids frantically start to talk to her. Heads together, leaning in, both now try to hear. He puts the phone on speaker, so they can listen and talk at the same time.

But he feels odd to be listening to what she says to them.

He gets out of the car. Closes the door. Stands nearby as he gives them space to speak with their mother.

It's warm outside, even in the dark. He can hear people moving around inside one of the cars near him. Shifting uncomfortably in their seats. He can hear someone snoring lightly in the church. He hears insects flying, buzzing the church and the cars, insects newly risen from the layer of mud that covers the delta.

"Dad," his son says, opening the door, twenty minutes later. "Mom wants to talk to you."

He gets back into the driver's seat. Takes the phone. Turns off the speakerphone. "Keep going north," she says to him. "Don't come back this way. It's not safe. It's worse than what they're saying. Much worse. I can't even get out of this building."

"Okay," he says.

She's crying.

"Thank you," she says. "For getting them out."

He says in a moment, "It was only luck."

"Let me talk to the kids again," she seems to say, but he isn't sure. The phone has cut out. No signal. Connection lost.

He tells the kids. They sit silently. Then his son begins to cry, very quietly. His daughter stares out the window.

"Make way," he says, motioning them to move to the sides of the backseat. He crawls through the front seats, awkwardly, then lands between them, turning to sit. He reaches out to them. They sink into him, on each side.

All he can do is hold them.

"She's going to be okay," he whispers. "She's going to be okay."

They sit that way, father whispering, each pressed close together, sitting that way for quite some time.

It's strange. He knows he'd once cared about her. But for years he hasn't cared. And so what he feels now isn't clear. It's not that he doesn't want her to be alive. It's not that he isn't concerned about what happens to her next.

But he knows something. Now, seeing it unexpectedly amid the chaos.

He knows he does not miss her.

"She's going to be okay," he whispers to his children. Because that is what they need to hear.

But he knows now, sadly, finally, without any doubt, he knows that he no longer loves her.

• • •

A massive world, multidimensional, inhabited by creatures real and artificial, and some are in between, all accessed and controlled by kids hiding phones behind their big backpacks in the classroom.

The meeting of investors trying to make more money, investing profits, together via video conference identifying tax havens, legal structures, offshore holdings that can maximize their wealth.

The profiles of desperate men, others pious, others sad. The profiles of people looking for pleasure of every deviant and deranged kind. The profiles of women looking to be loved, simply, no touching, none of that, simply talk to me and, sometimes, will you please make me smile?

In the air on the hill, the smell of rot is stronger. People, the bodies in the mud, beginning to decay. But the mud continues to dry. Enough that people test the area at the bottom of the hill. A group uses the father's hammer and screwdrivers to strip boards from the walls of the church. They place the boards onto the mud. A rope has been found. One man is tied around the chest. Step by step, board after board, the man with the rope is able to cross the drying mud. In ten minutes, he reaches the shoulder of the highway.

The boards sink some in places. But the mud is almost solid now. No longer does it suck people down inside it.

Some people without vehicles leave the hill immediately. Pairs or people alone. Walking single file across the narrow row of boards, stepping delicately, lightly, at the ready to jump forward or back or just away. The memory of what could happen in this mud has not disappeared for anyone.

But most people stay on the hill for now. Assessing. Talking about where they'll go. How far they'll have to walk. They are forty miles from the city north of here. The radio says it survived, the wave having dissipated before it reached that far.

The people with cars on the hill know they can't yet leave. Their cars would bog down in the mud between here and the highway.

In the morning, another helicopter circles them. A military helicopter: a person in uniform leans out the aircraft's door. He or she waves to them. They wave back. The person in the helicopter moves their arms and hands. Giving some sort of signal. Thumbs-up or stay put or you must get out of here. No one knows. The helicopter flies away.

More people walk across the wooden path to the highway. Turning north.

As he crosses, one man accidentally steps off the boards, stumbling to the left as a board sinks under his foot; three steps he takes, now four and five and six as he tries to regain his balance, his momentum finally carrying him twenty feet away from the path. He's begun to scream, his feet sinking, then his legs, the mud is already above his knees.

In some places, the mud is still that deep.

The woman with him yells for him to stop, don't move. He has his hands up in the air as if balancing. The mud has reached midway up his thighs.

The rope is brought down the hill. Someone throws it to the woman, who then throws the end of the rope to the man.

He's panicking. Can't reach it.

She throws it again.

The mud is near his waist.

She throws the rope again. Yelling for him to grab it. *Just grab it. It's next to you, please grab it.*

He finally does. But he still can't see her. His back to her. Sinking slowly. And listing forward. Swinging his arms carefully, as if he's simply lost his balance.

He manages to reach the rope, though, and tie it around his chest, and the woman begins to pull.

For a few minutes, it seems that he is moving toward her. Leaning back. Maybe, somehow, she'll be able to pull him from the mud.

No one joins her on the boards to help. Out of fear for themselves. She must know this. Understand it. She doesn't ask for help from anyone.

It's dusk now. She's sat down on the boards. Her feet are dug into the wood and the dirt and the mud in front of her. Leaning back against the rope. Pulling on the man.

He's sunk down to his armpits now. Already the rope where it's tied around his body has sunk beneath the mud.

He's talking. His lips and mouth are moving. And whether he's whispering to himself or whispering to her or saying prayers or cursing the world or telling the woman how and why he loves her, no one knows. The others can only watch, from a distance.

Even after his head is gone and the sun has barely set, the woman sits there still, on the boards, pulling hard, leaning back, hanging on to that thin rope.

• • •

Dinner tables in the finest restaurants, the patrons' faces lit so brightly by the screens they hold before them.

· · ·

Two days later, the people with cars begin to put down more boards, stripping the church of more siding, the mold-covered boards laid out, one after another. A ramp, or is it a bridge, linking this hill to the highway.

The father uses his hammer to pry loose the siding, his kids near him, holding the boards as they come free, then stacking them nearby. Other people pick up the boards and walk them down the hill. Putting them in place.

He and his kids were the first car up the hill and so will be the last to leave.

The cars, one by one, cross the white wooden path the people made. The boards sink a little with each car that crosses. Water pools on some boards, other boards sink into the dirt that, with the pressure of the cars, is once more turning into mud.

"You're both going to sit up front for now," he says to his kids. "And you're going to listen to everything that I say."

They pass the tombstones in the cemetery as he lets the car begin to roll, inching down the hill, moving with gravity more than the engine.

"If we start to sink, I'll tell you," he says. "And then we'll climb out the windows. Onto the roof. And we'll be fine. No matter what, we'll be fine."

The kids both nod. Staring forward now.

The tires touch the first of the boards, the wheels for a moment spinning, then they grip the wood. He keeps going, the car rocking, listing now, to the left. He feels one board give way. He hears another board crack and pop. But he keeps the car moving forward.

Don't get stuck, he tells himself. *Move.*

The car is listing more. The left side of the path is ruined. He realizes there are bodies in the mud. Mounds, he'd thought, just dirt. But they are bodies, bent over, faces in the mud, backs hunched as they desperately tried to lift themselves from the suffocating earth.

He grips harder on the leather steering wheel, while his foot taps harder at the accelerator. *A little faster. Just a little faster.*

The kids are starting to yell. Unintentionally. Not even aware. It's a low moan, rising, guttural. They both are reaching for him, trying to jump over to his side of the car.

"No, stay there," he tries to yell, "stay there." But his voice is just a whisper.

The car keeps sinking to the left and he's pushing against the kids with his right arm, the car seeming to sink more with every second, his children held away from him and now he's pushing harder on the gas, maybe that's the wrong move, maybe that will only dig them deeper into the mud, he sees it out his window, wet here, liquid, as the car slides off what boards remain, another body coated in a layer of mud, two bodies coated in a layer of mud, an adult holding tightly to her child, a bas-relief image of a horror he thought they'd avoided but instead he knows they'll sink, the car will sink, he will sink, his kids will sink with him, joining the mud-encased remnants of a disaster too great to comprehend, but all that matters is he'd thought he'd kept them safe.

He wants to scream.

He wants to cry.

He wants to hold his children.

They reach the shoulder of the highway. Suddenly moving fast. The car righting itself as it hits the drier land.

The kids are screaming, happy, he is screaming too, as the car reaches the asphalt highway, dry pavement. The kids bounce in their seat, screaming happily, *"Daddy, daddy, daddy!"* Again.

And again.

He stops the car. Reaches to hug them both, both of them at once. They slap hands. They hug again. He needs water. His daughter dances. His son looks down, around, finds the phone. Looks at it. Then hands it to his father.

"It's still not working," his son says.

His sister stops her dance. She drinks water. The boy does too.

"I know," the father says, slowly taking the phone from his son. "But we'll just keep checking."

The kids both nod. He tells them to move to the backseat. Buckle up.

In the night, as his children slept, he heard the news reports. Three buildings back in the city that didn't collapse in the first onslaught of the water. But they finally did collapse. Hers included. The reporter used its name. Of the building where she lived. The building where his kids lived half the time.

She had even texted him. *Oh god. My god. I think we're finally done.*

The water simply took some time to finally bring those buildings down.

Dumb luck. The timing. It's just dumb luck. That his kids are here.

On other stations, he heard more baseball. News about movies. News about business and diplomacy and war.

The world continues.

He can't quite figure out how to tell the kids that their mother died.

They'll drive to the nearby city. Regroup. Then head much farther north. The city where he lived when he was a child. An industrial city. Dying. Where his parents have remained.

The man takes a breath. Another. Then looks around. In the mirror, he sees his children doing the same. As if only now are they able to look at what's around them.

And to the left and right, to the north and south, all they can see is this flat highway, dry with dirt, covered with abandoned cars and wrecked trucks, and everywhere, as far as they can see, are the bodies of the people who did not survive.

• • •

Phone calls, texts, video communication, medical history, photo sharing, news, jokes, porn, sports, movies, research, books. Just so many books.

All sent simultaneously across this ether of electronic devices. All of it operating despite the heat, or the rain, or earthquakes, or tsunamis. Even blackouts don't shut it down, people switching seamlessly from wall power to battery pack, or even simply switching from a computer or a TV to the sleek black phone in their rough hands; the cell towers that dot each landscape, densely urban or very rural, have all been tagged as a priority for electricity, a choice deemed a necessary protection against an unimaginable chaos, one of many choices that create a sense for everyone that this ether of so much connection is not man-made but divine.

Still they laugh. Sitting on those couches.

He wonders. She wonders.

Even as they laugh.

There's a lightness to it all. Something they can feel. Something that seems to shimmer.

Rings on their fingers. This can only end in sadness.

CHAPTER 5

THE INVESTOR

The checkerboard tile floors still lie flat at the street corner. The walls of the small buildings are gone. Only the ground floors now remain. It's a small town, rural, with three tile floors, each one covering the entirety of the lots where they were built.

Commercial buildings long ago destroyed. By tornado or inattention or storm. There's no way to know for sure.

Few people are left in this town. The courthouse square is overgrown. A deputy wanders out of the courthouse itself, using a fire exit. The main doors have swollen shut from so much leaking rain.

Near the highway, just a few miles from here, the shopping center glows all day and night. Cars and trucks and even tractors, they make their way to the parking lot. Drawn there, forced there, this collection of shining, massive boxes is the center of this town's commerce.

Decades in the making. Now reality across hundreds and thousands of rural and forgotten places.

• • •

She never thinks about why she pays people to have sex with her. She doesn't question it. Debate it. Doesn't feel guilt or shame or insecurity.

She likes the way she has sex.

So she keeps on doing it.

Outside her window, clouds of dandelion seeds float through the air.

She asks her analysts about a coastal country on the other side of the world.

The analysts run through metrics on the history of developments along that country's shoreline. Small towns, large resorts, fishing villages, massive industrial ports. All built in areas easily identified as at risk. At risk of flooding in some sort of disaster. A typhoon or an earthquake. But also at risk from the slowly rising water.

"Who are the insurers on the big developments?" she asks. She's turned completely to her window. Watching the dandelions blow by, a near fog of white seeds, or are they spores, she wonders, but doesn't need to know.

The analysts list the names of the insurance companies that protect billions of dollars in large investments along that coastline.

She says, "I want contracts against them all."

The dandelion clouds begin to blow straight up, riding a thermal or a breeze. They've been blowing through the city for days.

She didn't like the man she had last night. He moved too fast. He was too loud. It left her less satisfied than before she'd started. She'd returned to her apartment early. Going home instead to be alone.

"The rural provinces," she says. "The poor cities along the coast. Do they issue their own debt?"

She hears the faint tapping on the laptop keyboards. Quiet, though. As if the analysts knew to buy laptops as silent as this room in which they work.

"Yes," one of the analysts says. "Many billions' worth."

"Bet against it," she says.

She'd like to have that young man again. With his story of wearing his cousin's dress. She'll make a call soon. And stop by a store on the way home. Buy him something nice to wear.

The analysts move through other countries along that coast. Near the equator. The conversation about one of the island nations takes nearly a full hour. The opportunities are just that large.

"Tomorrow," she says, "we need to focus on the near term. What we're discussing now is all for the future. Tomorrow, I want to focus on today."

The dandelion clouds start to shift again, beginning to blow west, then down, but for a moment, as the direction of the wind changes, the dandelion clouds outside her windows have stopped moving, frozen in place sixty stories in the air, each white seed suspended here; she stares from one to another and to another. Held in place. As if time has stopped. And for that moment she thinks that she could identify each seed, all of the millions of them, she could study and remember each one.

The heat lifts them again, they move upward, even higher into the sky.

"Herbicides," she says. "Who knows anything about herbicides?"

• • •

The suburbs all have a chosen facade. Mostly tan or mostly brown, mostly wooden or mostly brick. The convenience stores distinguished from the doctors' offices only by the small signs allowed to be hung discreetly on the front of buildings.

A dull and numbing ubiquity parading as an understated, planned aesthetic.

Teenagers roam in family cars, buying beer behind the gas station. Buying painkillers behind the mall. Finding half-finished subdivisions abandoned during a banking crisis, now shelters for small parties, forced sex, addictions some will try to conquer before there's a worse descent.

Schools overflowing with more students than they can handle, fed by a constant influx of corporate transfers, young couples, people fleeing the problems of the cities, be they real or just imagined.

• • •

She never thinks about the morality of making money off natural disasters. The rules say she can. There's nothing about what she does that is illegal.

Her job is to make money. Increase it. Multiply it. Add to the pile she and her team and her company already have.

She doesn't question this.

59

She's very good at it.

So she makes as much as she possibly can.

She didn't always make her money off these disasters. For years, she made it other ways. But the disasters kept presenting themselves. More times than she could ignore.

She's already made the company a billion dollars off the disaster in the Gulf. But her bosses have long since learned not to congratulate her on any investment that pays off. Over the years, each of them has done that once. Showing up in her office and starting to clap or even cheer.

She winced. She looked away. Asked finally, "Is there anything else you came to say?"

Now, they only wander by. Trying hard to seem casual.

This time, the oldest one comes by her office. Gray hair. Tan. Big class ring. Gold wedding band. His wristwatch might cost fifty thousand dollars. He's come into her office. Sits on her couch. Trying hard to be quiet. But he isn't quiet. Not by nature.

That he is so obviously trying to be quiet somehow makes him louder.

"Yes?" she says. Turning to him. Hand on the elevated desk.

"Good week," he says.

In a moment, she says, "Yes."

He pauses. Nods. Soon says, "I went through the new additions to your portfolio." Again, he pauses. He shifts loudly. "With anyone else, I wouldn't allow such risk."

"Is it the risk?" she asks. "Or the prospect of making money off such terrible things?"

He shifts in place again. Glances around the room. It's almost empty except for the couch and three chairs and her elevated desk. On the walls are huge photographs of old cities captured in the night, lit bright with electric streetlamps, cars and trolleys and horse-drawn carriages all crowded along broad avenues.

"Well," he says now. "They are certainly terrible possibilities. But it's not as if you created these possibilities. And," he starts, laughing suddenly, "it's not as if we want these things to happen."

She hates the abrupt, disruptive sound of awkward laughter.

She says to him, "Of course we want these things to happen. It's an assumption in the model."

He looks around. Smiling obviously.

She hopes he doesn't laugh again.

"That sounds almost evil," he says finally, lightly, trying to joke.

She shakes her head. "I don't believe in evil."

"Not a churchgoer?" he asks, the awkward smile. Again, he shifts in place.

"No," she says.

He nods. He doesn't speak for a long moment. But he continually repositions his feet and arms.

"We need to dress up the new portfolio," he says finally. "Not change it. But put some other types of investments in there. In case some regulator, some detective, a reporter, looks at it more closely than we'd like."

She says, "You want to adorn it with the appearance of greater hope."

He stares at her. The awkward smile fades. He's not sure how to take what she has said.

Most people around here, she knows, they joke. This is all a game.

"I suppose," he says, looking away. "Yes."

"Send me your suggestions," she says. "I see no need for this. But, as long as you don't undermine the model's inherent purpose, certain changes may be fine."

His voice is louder suddenly. Not loud. But louder. "Would you ever want to talk about all this over a drink?" he asks.

She stares at him. "No."

He nods. He looks around. In a moment, he says, "I'll have someone send suggestions."

She shakes her head. "I won't look at them unless they come from you."

He's quiet.

"Just this week, I have made you a massive amount of money off the deaths of many thousands of people in the Gulf," she says. "Around the world, we're betting on the resultant deaths of many, many more. There's a ratio, in fact. A correlation between the number of dead and the amount of money we will make. The correlation is not linear. It's exponential. Returns that grow by several orders of magnitude as the death toll rises. I can show it to you if you'd like. It's right here on my computer. But if you don't approve of this reality, if you don't want me operating in this territory, you will need to tell me so. Tell me. Clearly. Say it," she says. "Say it now."

He stares at her. Even though, she realizes, he very much does not want to.

She says to him again, "Say it now."

He stands. Looks around the room. "Okay," he says. "Yes. I will send you my suggestions."

"Anything else?" she asks.

He shakes his head. "Nothing," he says.

It's another minute before he leaves.

But she's already turned back to her computer.

• • •

Vast walls of scaffolding built within the city itself, pipes and wooden platforms not intended to aid in repairing the deteriorating buildings but erected only to protect passersby from the crumbling facades of the stores and apartments and skyscrapers they walk past.

Whole city blocks fenced off, chain-link, razor wire, public housing built many decades ago to cordon off the poor and brown, housing that's decrepit now, wasted, and no one can justify its use.

Whole neighborhoods, for miles, not a grocery store, no real food for sale, just brightly packaged sustenance. Small children eat it in their strollers.

• • •

She's bought a dress for him. A white one. And his own bra and panties. Pink. With small flowers. He is a beautiful boy. Sixteen, probably. Though he promises he is older.

She's dressed him, applied eyeliner. She paints his lips a darker pink. Adds a little shine. She has perfume for him. She combs his long hair out, lays it across his shoulders.

He sits watching her. Only breathing slowly.

She says to him, quietly, "I want you to feel pretty."

His legs are shaven. His whole body is. He's taken care of that on his own.

"Stand," she says.

She is behind him as he stands at the mirror. She takes his hands, moves them up and down his body. Across the cool material of the dress. The bra beneath it. She guides his hands to the dress's hem. Lifts it slightly. Finds the panties. Runs his fingers along the thin top edge, letting his fingers slide inside them.

She lays him down on the bed. She wears jeans. A loose T-shirt. She puts her hair up, pinning it behind her head.

She spreads his legs. Pushes the dress up to his belly button.

"Do you wish you were a girl?" she asks him.

He says, "Sometimes."

"Do you wish that I could fuck you?" she asks.

"Yes," he says.

She unzips her jeans. Slides them off. Takes off her underwear. But leaves the T-shirt on.

She's between his legs. He's hard and she moves him so that his legs are spread but he can be inside her. She pushes, her hips working him.

He lets his head fall back as she does this. His knees rise. She unbuttons the dress so she can see his bra. Pushes one cup down. Sucks on his bare nipple.

"And when," he whispers, pausing, leaning back even more, his legs spread as his knees move, "when is the first time you had sex?"

People have asked. But she has never answered. Just guided them on to whatever she wanted next.

But she likes this boy. How quiet he is. How pretty he is. How he lets her dress him up. How he lets her fuck him like he is a girl.

"I was twenty-five," she says. "No one had ever tried. Or ever offered."

"That's not possible," he says.

She rocks forward and back, steadily, again and again.

"Yes, it is," she says. "Back then I wasn't pretty. I wasn't beautiful. I was just very plain."

"You're not plain," he says. "You're beautiful."

"Yes," she says, sliding a bra strap off his shoulder, taking a moment to suck lightly on his nipple, speaking words between each lick or kiss, "I am now. But I wasn't then."

He rocks back, with each push, legs spread, eyes closed. Panties pulled aside, dress pushed up and bra askew. He's a girl. He feels it. She does. He's a girl.

"And so," she says quietly, "I read a book. And while I read I touched myself. Which I'd done. But this was different. The book had prostitutes in it. A man who bought them. Brought them to his apartment in a building high up in the sky. Every night. And I touched myself. And came. But this time, for the first time, I realized I could come again. Four or five or six times. I could come as many times as I wanted."

He's breathing hard. Lying back. Eyes closed. Being fucked. He's always wanted to be fucked.

"And the next night I went online," she says. "Found a place. And ordered up a man."

He's breathing even harder.

She leans close to him, near his ear, working him. This time, it's all for him.

She whispers, "Can I come inside you?"

His lips move. But he doesn't speak.

"Can I come inside you?"

His lips move. No words. He nods. Nods again. "Yes," he finally whispers, more breath than word. "Please come."

• • •

64

Beach communities destroyed. Not by hurricanes or earthquakes or even by massive waves. Instead, the beach is simply moving. Slowly disappearing into the surf. Rows of houses that were once located a block or two from the beach are now, years later, positioned on the beachfront, their porches looking out on the remnants of other homes, built tall on massive stilts, now battered by the surf.

Homes of the very wealthy, or rented by the rich, or rented by the middle class, the working class. Escapes for each of them. A place to escape their normal lives.

The front steps of the houses all descend, staircases that meet the waves. The houses, in the sunset, forty of them in various stages of destruction, they are an almost beautiful backdrop, silhouettes of what once was, the sun behind them slowly dropping out of view.

• • •

She's gotten quite focused on that boy. Seeing him a few times a week. He lets her dress him. His shaved body gets smoother every time, so that the panties she slides onto him and the bra she clips at his back and the dress she buttons carefully, it all makes him feel like a girl. His hair is long. She gets to brush it. And when he comes inside her, his legs spread, rocking back as she pushes against him, every time it's instead like she's come inside of him.

So she'll see him again.

She folds investments into the model. Municipal debt swaps, the shorting of insurance stocks. The concepts are simple. She's not entirely sure why more people are not doing this.

Maybe it's the idea that something about this is deeply wrong.

Maybe there's a feeling that this must ultimately be illegal.

Probably at least some people would find this to be quite scary.

Her analysts list the company names. City names. Provincial capitals. Population stats and demographics.

"And so where are we on short-term options?" she asks eventually.

"We have agricultural scenarios," one analyst says.

"The death of home landscaping services?" she asks him.

He shakes his head, pausing, then smiling some.

She likes it that he found her to be funny.

"There's not enough of a market in home services," he says now. "Too small. But in food there's a market we should like. We have a model that anticipates escalating growth in pricing. But also there's the entirety of the supply chain. Warehousing, grocery stores, restaurant supply, fast-food franchising. Costs will increase, in some cases very dramatically."

She nods. On her screen, she's moving through the model that they've sent her. In a moment, she says, "Yes."

"You'll see calculations for here and for abroad," another analyst says.

"Yes," she says.

"And there's land," says another analyst. "So that we have a series of targeted purchases—insurance, commodity contracts, muni debt, water rights, and land leases—all tied to key stages of an inevitable loss of farmable or livable land."

She stares at the numbers. Calculates on her screen. Runs scenarios in her mind. In a moment, she says, "Yes."

Outside her window, the sky is turning dark.

"Also," one of the analysts is saying, even as the woman turns to watch the storm moving quickly toward her window, "I saw a story about a city. An industrial city. West of here. And how it's been abandoned."

The woman is standing very close to her window now, feeling the heat emanating from the glass, the sky turning black, rain starting now, and lightning. "I've heard of the place," she says. "But if it's already been abandoned, what is there to bet against?"

"Actually, there are two halves to the city," the analyst says. "Twin cities, really. And the other half, which is still populated, there are signs. It's starting to fail as well."

The storms, they come quickly. Dark and filled with lightning, and she assumes the tornado warnings have started to ring out. "How long could one half survive," the woman says, watching lightning flashes that seem mere

66

blocks away, even as thunder vibrates silently against the window, "while the other half continues to fail?"

"Right," says the analyst.

"Right," says the woman.

Rain sprays hard against the glass, blurring everything. She presses her hand against it. Cooling already, the water washing away the heat.

"I'd like to visit this place," the woman says.

"When?" one of them asks.

She has both hands against the glass now. Water spraying just an inch away. She says, "As soon as we possibly can."

• • •

The disconnected parking lots, some linked by short roads leading from one store to a gas station, but others blocked off for no apparent reason. A patchwork of asphalt and squares of grass, a stray tree, a crew of men putting mulch out, it's not clear why. The three shrubs and two trees are barely alive. But some property owner many hundreds of miles away has checked a box, doing something he thinks is right, *We landscape that parking lot we've always owned.*

To walk from one parking lot to another has become almost impossible, even though the distance isn't far. Hopping curbs, passing through broken fences. Places where walking was never considered.

There is trash at every step, foam cups and plastic bags, and there's a syringe and a beer can, and there's a bottle of an undetermined brand or purpose, the sun or rain or wind having stripped it of all its markings.

The remnants of stray people who once wandered through here, a place no one was ever meant to go.

The atrium above them dims just slightly.

Cleaning people have started working in the bar near the lobby.

But still they talk.

He wants very much to kiss her.

He's not sure what she thinks. But he knows this is what he wants.

She has blue eyes, he realizes. Something he'd never realized.

Clear and bright and blue. He can't stop thinking about her eyes.

CHAPTER 6
THE STRANGER

Symphonies gone bankrupt.

Museums unable to meet even their much-diminished payrolls.

Colleges combining: each a hundred years old, they now merge their small enrollments, one last effort to stay open another year.

• • •

Alone in his room, her younger son would use a steak knife to slowly cut a line along the inside of his thigh. It started not long after his older brother's first trip into rehab.

The parents hid the knives, and so he found the razors, snapping them from their plastic handles. The parents hid the razors, and so he found his dad's tools, selecting putty knives with hard corners and box cutters still sharp. The parents hid the tools, and so he took a wire hanger, unwinding it to expose the rough steel tip, pressing it back and forth on the brick patio, slowly sharpening it before taking it to his room.

The infection, the madness, it ran full force throughout the house. Mother and father in stages of denial for months, or was it years? Always so many steps behind. Identifying drinking, when the problem was already drugs. Identifying violence, when the problem was already self-abuse.

The order of events, even now, she can't quite recreate it in her mind. With her husband, probably, they could piece together the moments in a linear timeline.

But what's the point in that?

Tell yourself you'd do it better. Tell yourself you'd be on top of it. Tell yourself it'd be bad, but not as bad for you.

Then take your days and weeks and years and turn them inside out. Waking in the lobby of a mental health facility as the sun begins to set outside, your husband, brightly bruised around the face and neck, sleeping nearby on the hard floor. Your younger son, kicked out of school while you are with the older at a rehab facility in a distant state, day after day of painful, cold, and pointless therapy with and without your child. Your older son, who's back home, and, as you focus on putting a tracking device on his car, he's in his room now shooting heroin.

No one trains you for this, a therapist finally said. *No one tells you how to parent. Not even how to parent the best of children.*

He is the best of children, she responded.

Her husband turned to her.

No, the therapist said. *He's not. Not anymore. But maybe, somehow, we can work to get him back.*

"The demons won," her husband says now. On the porch.

How long has he been out here?

The demons were his metaphor.

But it's not one she ever bought.

Still, he used that phrase all the time. *We're not at war with our son. We're at war with the demons who've overtaken him.*

"There is no such thing as demons," she says now.

She looks at him. He's drunk. She can see it in his eyes. Watery, and his face seems bloated. When she sees him, if she looks close, she can see the face of her son.

He shakes his head. Crying now.

Everyone's always crying.

"Don't," he says.

She remembers that he's been out here for an hour. More. They'd been talking. About their older son. But she can't remember anything that they've said.

70

She drinks. Swallows. "You can sink into your notions of demons taking over that boy," she is saying now. "But that is not what happened. It was chemicals. In his brain. There since he was born. Predetermined, predestined. This was DNA."

He shakes his head. "Please don't."

Only in his face, her husband's, can she clearly see her son before he died.

"Maybe for once we could talk about our other son," she says, exhaling, the vapor of gin, it crosses her eyes as she now blinks. "And how the fuck we're going to find him."

He stands, slowly.

"Time to go," she says. "Right? Time to take one of your fucking walks. No time, though, to talk about him. You had two children, you know. Not one."

They have hired a private detective, of course. A few of them. In the years since their youngest son ran away. There have been rumors. Claims that he's been sighted. But nothing more.

Her husband leaves the porch, walking down the steps, hand on the rail. Drunk. Once more disappearing into darkness.

In truth, he talks about their younger son all the time. She knows this. His sadness about the boy leaving is no less than hers. She knows that too.

Behind her, a house on the hillside a half a mile away burns brightly in the night. A huge house—as it burns, she thinks it looks like a fort that's been attacked. The stars in the sky are washed away in the light of the growing fire.

There's a misery to the repetition. How mental illness cycles endlessly. A force, a weight that pushes down, clouding everything it can touch.

The boys became strangers to their mother. To their father. Finally, they weren't even ghosts. Instead they became people their parents didn't recognize. Or had ever known.

Of course, the woman is a stranger too now. A stranger even to herself.

• • •

Libraries funded below a minimal level. Books sold at weekend sales in the library parking lot. Or discarded to save space. The tables on the first floor host the homeless who manage to behave, or young children waiting for their parents to pick them up after the library closes at seven.

• • •

Each spring has gotten worse. After six years of drought, subdivisions like this one have seen fires spread across the hillsides. The hills, it seems, are magnets for the flames. Lightning is the worst of it. Hitting dry landscapes of dying brush.

On the news, they say *tinderbox.*

The insurance companies, most of them, found exceptions in their policies to deny homeowners the coverage they thought they'd bought. Governments stepped in, with ten cents on the dollar.

Other insurance companies, the very small ones, simply bankrupted themselves in the face of all the claims.

And so, there's very little incentive for anyone to move.

Except, of course, the fires.

It would take an unprecedented wind to push the fire this way. A wind they've never had.

"What's wrong?" she asks him.

He's walked by her, nodding some, turning to go upstairs.

"What's wrong?" she asks again.

He stops on the bottom step.

"What?" she asks.

He turns to her. "I'm not sure how to answer," he says.

She shakes her head, just slightly. "Why?"

In a moment, he lets himself sit down on the steps, looking toward the big living room. "The last time we spoke," he says. "I mean." He pauses. Staring down. "It was very hard."

She nods. Nods again. Says in a moment, "Yes, it's very hard."

He turns his head toward her.

She's nodding. Nodding hard now. Lips tight. "Harder on you, of course," she says.

72

He stares at her.

"Always," she says. "Always this is harder on you."

He says, quietly, "I meant what you said to me. On the porch. It was hard to tolerate."

"On the porch?" she says, voice rising. "What I said on the porch? Oh. That's what you're upset about? You got your feelings hurt? I was hard to tolerate?" She shakes her head. Her arms are crossed, tightly. "Let me apologize. For your feelings and how they hurt. And my role. My essential responsibility for how bad and awful you always feel."

He stares.

"Why is it that I get all the blame and no support?" she says, arms crossed tighter. "Why is it that I can't feel safe here anymore? Why is it that every misstep of mine is thrown back into my face?"

He stares.

"And you have nothing to say," she says. "Always. Nothing to say. Nothing to do. No help to offer me. No love. No care. Just nothing."

He stares.

"Could you say something nice to me?" she asks, nearly yelling. She's turned red, eyes wet. "Could you say something kind?"

When she's this way, her husband can see pure shadows of what she once looked like. The shadows are so beautiful.

He starts to speak, pauses. Looks away. Looks back at her. "I would like to support you," he says. "I would like to love you. But you're impossible to reach."

She shakes her head. "And again, that's clearly my fault."

His head falls slowly, staring down now. At his feet.

"Always," she says, "it is my fault."

He starts to speak, says something maybe, but she cannot hear it. Or maybe his words simply have no force or sound behind them. So that now he looks only like a man sitting on the steps, head in his hands, whispering silently to himself.

• • •

Grand elementary schools built with aspirations of educating a new generation of young children. Now half empty, or is it two thirds, roofs leaking, gyms unusable, cafeterias infested as if there were no solution to the matter.

Neighbors flee. Parents run. Only the poorest stay behind. Without the voice or means or wherewithal to make any sort of change.

• • •

The fire is near their house now. The neighbor's home is totally ablaze. The neighbor who'd had the generator and the baby. She watched them leave a week ago. A moving van. And both their cars.

The caravan of abandonment. Repeated so many times by people here.

The wind has finally shifted. A turn deemed impossible by the experts. On hearing of this development, scientists speculate that the fire itself changed the course of the wind and, with it, the wall of flames.

The house next door burns bright. Like a castle that's been stormed and plundered, now left to burn like all the other conquered homes before it.

"We need to go," her husband says.

Over the last few days, he's emptied their home of anything of value. Financial or sentimental. Photos. Books. A painting they bought together in a delta city many years ago.

She tried to find something to keep from each of her boys' rooms. A stuffed animal. A blanket. A pop-up children's book high up on a forgotten shelf.

She couldn't.

But her husband swept through the boys' rooms, putting a last few items in a cardboard box.

She doesn't notice what he grabs.

She's found herself concluding that it would be better for all of it to burn.

The smell of smoke is strong.

"We need to go," he yells to her from outside.

She makes her way out the front door. "Where are we going?" she asks, standing on the porch.

He's in the driveway. "I'm not sure," he says. "Please, let's get in the car."

She stands still. Looking toward the approaching line of fire.

She can feel the heat. A different heat. Above the heat in the air and the heat from the sun. Something different than the constant heat they've had for these many years.

"Amazing that you can feel the fire," she says. "Even this far away."

She's watching the flames begin to cross the dead and yellow grass.

He's standing near her. "We need to go."

She watches. "Where?" she asks again.

He shakes his head. "I don't know. But we must leave."

She watches.

"One of the detectives," her husband says. "He called. He thinks he's found our son."

She leans her head back. Seeing thick smoke across all the sky. It's begun to block the sun. Mid-morning dusk.

In a minute, she asks, "Where?"

He tells her.

She nods. "That's a city far from here," she says.

"Yes."

"A dying city."

"Yes."

"What is he doing there?" she finally asks.

"It's not clear."

She stares at her husband now. Maybe it's the first time she's truly looked at him in years. "It's not clear? Or you won't tell me?"

"We have to go," he says. "The road will be covered in fire."

"Tell me," she says.

"The fire is coming this way," he says.

"Drugs?" she asks. "Prostitution?"

He's looking past her shoulder, toward the neighbor's home. Burning. The yard, the trees, all now burning too.

"Tell me," she says.

He looks at her. "Yes." He turns away. Back toward the front door. He walks up the steps. Pulls the door shut. "Yes," he says. "That and more."

She leaves the porch. Walking toward the car. Getting in. In a moment, he sits down in the seat next to her. Engine starting. Flames a hundred feet away.

"I have to go there," she says.

"I do too."

"I don't want you to go with me," she says. Which isn't true. She knows this. But she needs for him to say, again, that he wants to go with her.

"I am going also," he says.

He's backing the car down the driveway, quickly. Turning the car now, using the wide circle in the driveway; they're headed away from the house and the fire. Their home, it will burn soon, but she doesn't care. She thinks he probably doesn't either. Fire has been spreading through that house for years. Burning everything and everyone who once lived there.

They just never saw the flames.

• • •

A theater, nearly two hundred years old, is easily torn down. Rotted anyway. From the rainfall that poured for so many years through the gilded dome of a towering, decaying roof.

The musicians who had played there, the actors and actresses who once performed, the speeches long ago delivered, poetry read aloud, movies played. Funds were raised. During the war the stage was lined with beds.

Now gone.

Memories offer no protection. They are only a series of moments that happened in the past.

A small notebook falls from his pocket. She picks it up. Asks if she can read from it. He says yes. Instantly. Something he's never said to anyone.

She moves through the pages. Struggling to read his handwriting.

Usually, he tells her, *it's just things I've seen. Ideas I might write about next week. Or many years from now.*

She turns pages. Smiling some when she glances at him.

She wants very much to kiss him. But, for now, she just reads the notes aloud. He helps her where she hesitates, unable to read his writing.

A man, she says as she reads, smiling now, looking at him, confusion, a question. *A man. Living in a city. A city that's been abandoned.*

PART 2

A STRANGER EVEN TO HIMSELF

He rises early. But not by choice. It's just that his mother always made him do so. Even before they crossed the border.

Wake, she'd say in Spanish. *It's time to pray.*

He no longer prays. But waking is a habit now made physical. Unavoidable. Fifty now.

A life of waste. Alone his entire life. Never a wife. Never anything like love.

He stares at the ceiling of his single room.

The residue of drugs. Gin. He feels them. Still running through his body.

A nausea. Sickness. He shakes and cannot sleep. Cannot stand.

There's nothing to stop this but more time. Here. Alone in bed.

He turns onto his side, pulls his knees up, slowly, as he tightly curls in upon himself.

CHAPTER 7
THE CAROUSEL OPERATOR

Cars line up, a quarter mile or more, waiting to turn into the massive parking lot surrounding the church.

People watch, late at night, hoping for the preacher to call their names.

Men and women in Sunday suit or dress, crossing through the brick path in the flower-lined median, waving to a friend before starting up the stone steps of the cathedral.

• • •

The carousel circles around him, lit gold and red and green, the colors blurring together against the night sky he can see between the horses and unicorns and sleighs as they revolve. Where he stands at the control panel, the gears of the carousel clatter wildly with each rotation, the diesel engine loud, but a sound that only joins the uproar of the small roller coaster nearby and the coin-toss games fifty feet away and the loud music playing from the haunted house behind the carousel, all of it combining with the screaming voices of the children tugging desperately at their parents and siblings and friends.

He hates this job.

Carousel operator for a traveling parking lot carnival. He's been doing this for a month. This his fourth city. Sleeping in a small tent pitched on slivers of forgotten grass along a series of huge parking lots. Paid in cash at the end of each stop. A share of the take, calculated by people he has no reason to trust.

He finishes loading another round of kids and parents onto the carousel. Hits the start button. Checks the timer. Closes his eyes.

Probably, he should be happy just to have a job.

He opens his eyes. Stares up at the sky through an opening in the roof at the center of the carousel. Hears each sound of each ride and game throughout this parking lot. Focuses for a moment on a barker calling for players. A basketball hitting a rim. The cars of the small roller coaster crashing down the metal rails. A girlfriend screaming as she swings.

Screaming happily.

He lowers his head. Looks around again. And between the horses and children moving around him, he sees that the guy running the teacup ride is having a seizure. He's shaking in place and his eyes are rolling back in his head and there's spit, white spit, coming from his mouth.

He's a teenager, like the carousel operator. Maybe nineteen. Maybe twenty. Black kid. They've never spoken.

The children walking past the black kid on the ground begin to stare. Point. And laugh. Some of them are doubled over laughing.

The black kid falls to the ground.

Still the carousel circles the operator. He isn't sure what to do. But no one is coming to help. He steps up onto the rotating platform, weaving through the stationary animals, then jumping to the ground. He's landed on the wrong side of the carousel, but runs around it, past the parents and kids all waiting in line. He gets to the teacups. Standing over the black kid and his seizure, is on the ground, shaking, eyes still in the back of his head.

The carousel operator leans over him. A crowd of people stand around.

Then the guy stops shaking. Goes still.

"Did he just fucking die?" someone asks.

The crowd is silent otherwise. The carnival sounds are quieter here, where the carousel operator leans over the body, the usually uncontrolled noise blocked out by the people all around him.

The guy is still on the ground. It's not clear if he's breathing. His face is covered in snot and white saliva. His eyes are closed. His hands are raised, but frozen, it seems. His legs are too. One knee is lifted. Frozen too, stiff, locked in place by the seizure.

The carousel operator thinks he should put his hand under the guy's nose. See if he is breathing.

"God damn it!" the guy on the ground suddenly screams. Eyes closed, still not moving, except for his mouth. He screams again, "God fucking damn it!"

People step back. The carousel operator stands.

In another moment, the guy on the ground opens his eyes. Slowly begins to lower his hands, move his legs. Retaking control of his body. He's yelling again. "Ep-uh-*lepsy!*"

The crowd begins to break apart, moving on. Parents of kids on the tea-cups are asking someone to make the ride stop. The carousel operator goes to the controls. Finds the shutoff. Is about to stop the ride.

"Don't you touch my fucking ride," the epileptic says to him, smiling as he stands. "No one touches my damn ride, okay? I'm an epileptic. Not a fucking retard."

The carousel operator has no idea what to say. He lifts his hands from the controls. He looks at the epileptic. Finally, the carousel operator says, in his quiet voice, "So you're okay?"

"You mean other than I almost swallowed my tongue?" the epileptic asks, moving to the controls. "Other than that, yep, I'm fan-fucking-tastic." He's slowing the ride down. Breathing hard. Wiping his face with his sleeve. "However, the latent effects of a slight and undiagnosed autism do still color my life perspective. Nor have I gotten laid in months. Not to mention," he says, wiping his face again, his sleeve damp with snot and sweat and spit, "I haven't had a goddamned beer all day."

The epileptic looks over toward the carousel. Says, in a moment, "Sir, you've got yourself a group of very unhappy patrons."

The carousel operator turns around. People are yelling at him from their seats in the sleigh, they're gripping frantically to the poles on which the horses and unicorns are mounted. From behind the fence lining the carousel, parents are waving wildly to their children, telling them to stay calm.

"I'd get those people some satisfaction right away," says the epileptic. "Then you and me, later, we'll see what we can do to get me a lady. And both of us a beer."

• • •

They stand on cue, all of them, rising without being asked, nodding without being asked, crossing their fingers over their chests, again without being asked. They begin to kneel now, the room filled with a low and wooden rumble as padded kneelers are unfolded from underneath each pew, the parishioners lowering themselves onto those padded planks. A minute later, the kneelers are tucked away again, once more discreetly positioned underneath each visitor to this church.

The people sit. They stand again. They repeat a phrase, the same phrase, an answer, a response, all of them, young and old, child and parent, they know these motions and these words by heart, it's as if they've known them since before they were even born.

• • •

The two of them head into town. Not the places near the shopping center where the carnival has set up. The epileptic wants to head into town. "The real town," he says to the carousel operator. "Where the people really live."

They hitch a ride in the back of a pickup truck. Riding along dark roads toward some bar the driver says they'll like.

"So let's talk seizures," the epileptic says, talking loudly as they sit with their backs to the truck's steel cab, the warm wind blowing all around them. "I may not have one for another year, I may have one before I finish this sentence." He looks up, at the sky above the trees around them. The carousel operator finds himself holding his breath. It's another moment before the epileptic starts talking again. "Either way, if you're a witness to another seizure, do me a favor. Shove something in my mouth. So I don't bite off my goddamn tongue. Okay?"

85

The carousel operator nods.

The epileptic nods too.

Behind them, the road winds slowly away, lost to the darkness and the trees. There are a few mailboxes along the road. But no lights of houses that they can see anywhere.

"What's the farthest away you've ever gone?" the epileptic asks.

The carousel operator names the places. He says, beneath the wind, "Drove north for five days just to get there."

"Damn," the epileptic says. "That's a good one. What the hell were you doing way up there?"

"Pitching fish," the carousel operator says quietly. "In a processing plant. Salmon."

The epileptic taps his hand on the side of the truck, nodding as he listens.

The carousel operator thinks he'd like to say more. He's not sure why. Usually, he hardly speaks at all. In a minute, he says, "Lived in a tent on a hill near a river. Worked seven days a week, twelve or sixteen hours a day."

"Damn," the epileptic says. "And isn't that the place where the sun doesn't go down?"

The carousel operator nods. "Not in the summer. It lasts a couple months."

"Damn," the epileptic says. "Didn't that fuck with your sleep?"

Wind blows hair all across the carousel operator's hard face. But he just lets it pass across his mouth and nose and eyes. "At first," he finally says. "But then, when you work that much, you can pretty much sleep anytime. Anywhere."

The truck bounces over a pothole in the road, their stomachs go empty, and for a moment it's like they fly.

"What's your story?" the epileptic asks. "I mean, what makes a guy go so far up there and do that sort of work?"

The carousel operator thinks about this for a minute. "Because none of it's where I'm from," he says, his quiet voice still somehow breaking through the noise of the wind. "All of it is somewhere else."

"Where are you from?" the epileptic asks.

The carousel operator tells him. "You know," he says, "in the northwest."

"Mountains and forests and shit like that?" the epileptic asks. "Supposed to be beautiful."

The carousel operator stares back at the road behind them, still disappearing into the night. "That's what people say. But it was just a big, dark city for me. A place where people worked at the port and where it seemed like I would end up working at the port too. Getting some girl pregnant. Moving into some apartment. Losing any picture of another life. Of being something else."

The carousel operator hasn't talked this much in many months. It makes his mouth ache a little. But somehow, this guy makes him talk.

The epileptic has picked up a small branch from the bed of the truck. He peels dead needles from the stick. One by one. Lifting them up into the air, then letting them fly. "So, okay," the epileptic asks, "tell me what else do you want from your days left on this earth?"

The carousel operator closes his eyes. The wind is warm, the cab of the truck even warmer. Still heated up from the sun that shone all day. He remembers being up north. He remembers a truck he rode in, hitchhiking along an empty peninsula, one night, like many nights, going from a bar to his tent near the camp, and he remembers that he loved to be away from home.

"What I want," the carousel operator says in that voice barely audible in the open, night drive, "is not to be where I am from."

The epileptic smiles. They drive a while. In a few minutes, the epileptic pats his new friend's knee. "I like that," he says.

The driver downshifts as they start up a low hill.

"Long way to go for a beer," the epileptic says.

"I was a bad person there," the carousel operator says, almost to himself.

"We've all been bad people," the epileptic says.

The carousel operator nods.

Wind blows over and around their heads. The sound of the engine rises as they mount the hill.

In a minute, the carousel operator turns to the epileptic. Facing him. They're sitting close together. He says softly, "I can promise you I was worse."

At the top of the hill, the truck begins to slow, turning off onto the shoulder of the road. They see a bar in an old wooden warehouse. Cars and trucks are parked in the dirt around it. The two of them hop over the side of the pickup truck. They land on the ground. Thank the driver. The carousel operator offers him a few dollars. The driver shakes his head, then the truck pulls away.

"So where are you from?" the carousel operator asks.

The epileptic smiles the wild smile he's got, crooked teeth and even in the light of the sign over the entrance to the bar, it's clear he needs to shave. "I can't possibly remember."

• • •

The priest moves forward, wearing her blue uniform or is it a costume, passing through the crowds of people pushing toward her. She's in the street. Walking toward the square. She touches everyone she sees, their hands or arms and some she touches their faces, which they press in her direction, begging, pleading, all they want is to be touched.

• • •

"This bar seems a designated gathering place for the injured and crippled," the epileptic says, pausing only long enough to drink from his cold bottle of beer. "It's like you've got to have at least lost a limb just to gain fair entry."

The carousel operator looks around. The epileptic's only barely exaggerating. Lost fingers on a waitress. A one-armed man at a table near the door. A woman and her boyfriend whose faces are scarred deeply from forehead to chin, their noses split and the woman is missing an eye.

"I mean," says the epileptic, "how the fuck did they both get matching scars?"

In a moment, his new friend offers slowly, "Maybe they were riding on the same tractor?" He's drinking beer too.

"My bet is they were going at it in some hidden stand of corn," the epileptic says, leaning close and almost whispering, "and then a god damned combine came charging through."

The epileptic has started laughing loudly.

His friend the carousel operator thinks it's funny too. But he can only barely smile.

He's a couple beers ahead of the epileptic.

He can't help counting. Where he grew up, you counted.

The bar is in a building that was once a warehouse for cotton. The ceilings are sixty feet high, and there's farm equipment everywhere. Rusted plows. A massive scythe. Bushels of cotton. The tables are wooden, built of planks seemingly stripped from a farmhouse or a barn. A ladder reaches all the way to the rafters. How can there be a ladder that tall?

"How much of this you think was brought in here as decoration?" the epileptic asks, looking around. "And how much was simply left here when someone decided this warehouse no longer served any functional agricultural purpose?"

The carousel operator looks around. Says quietly, "Not sure."

The bartender changes the channel on one of the televisions behind the bar. There's video from a helicopter. A city whose streets are being washed over with water. No sound. But there's music playing in the bar, some sort of blues. Dark and slow and loud. On the television, cars are barely visible in the water, on their sides, turned over. A few trees stand. There are bent streetlights and dangling utility poles. There are the shells of broken homes. There are buildings whose doors run with water. The video cuts to a river breaking through its banks. The video cuts to a lake overflowing an earthen wall. The video cuts to a highway, cars, being pushed aside by a heavy, low rush of thick and filthy water.

"What the fuck happened?" the epileptic asks.

His friend shakes his head.

"Do you have a phone?" the epileptic asks.

Once again, his friend shakes his head.

In the bar, some people watch the television. The bartender does. A few people sitting near them. But mostly the thirty or forty people here sit drinking their beer, staring toward one of the other televisions that show car racing, church sermons, and on one of the TV's there's baseball.

The kid and the epileptic watch a cell tower fall. A smokestack. An oil rig, in the Gulf, they see it slip into the water, steam and smoke and flames erupting, then extinguished. On the television, oil rises to the surface of the waves, the video now showing how it coats beaches and boats and animals.

"What the fuck happened?" the epileptic asks again.

The carousel operator only stares.

The epileptic turns to the bartender. An old guy, gray-haired, his pale face lined and sinking down toward his weathered neck. "What the fuck happened?" the epileptic asks him.

The bartender glances at him, then turns back to the television.

The epileptic leans toward his friend, the carousel operator. "God damned backwoods," he says. "Ask him what happened."

The friend doesn't understand. He shakes his head. "What do you mean?"

"You ask," the epileptic says. "That's the way it works."

The carousel operator shakes his head. "What?"

The epileptic smiles some. Pats his new friend on the arm. "You're a good man," the epileptic says.

The epileptic is black. His friend had forgotten that.

The carousel operator leans forward. Looking at the bartender. "What's going on there?" he asks and has to think to raise his voice. "On the TV."

The bartender glances at him. In a moment says, "This was days ago. Wake the fuck up. There was a hurricane. Then an earthquake. Which then combined," he starts, turning away, walking toward a back room, "with the unimaginable wrath of God."

The epileptic turns his head, looking around the room. At the people drinking beer. At the scarred man and his girlfriend playing pool and at the group playing darts. It's loud here, the music grinds, the epileptic still looking around the room.

"And they say *we* work in a carnival," the epileptic says.

The carousel operator glances around the room. The epileptic finishes his beer.

"How many people," the epileptic asks, "how many people you think died?"

His friend shakes his head again. Shrugs. "Don't know. A lot." He drinks. Says, "A hundred?"

The epileptic turns back to the television. More video of neighborhoods being washed over with water, homes collapsing, cars pushed side to side, against one another, people in boats overturned by the mess of debris in the water itself, a mass of boards and trees and people, made liquid by the water flowing everywhere.

"No, no," the epileptic says, shaking his head, staring at the TV, but now he closes his eyes, his voice almost a whisper, talking to himself or maybe it's that he prays. "That water, that violence," he says, "I'm telling you, that sort of thing killed thousands and thousands and thousands."

• • •

Candles burn, on altars, each one part of a carefully positioned arrangement.

A star, a circle, a cross, a square, the candles burn as the people talk, quietly, even as all of them close their eyes, reciting lines each reads from papers they hold in their hands.

• • •

A man, not much older than the two of them, now pushes up to the bar, asking for a beer. He's a big guy in a check shirt, and he's got a soaking load of dip in his front lip. The epileptic is pushed from his stool, almost falling on his friend, the carousel operator.

His friend thinks the epileptic will get mad. Push back. But he doesn't. He just rights himself, standing aside. Smiling. Waiting for the man to get his beer.

The carousel operator and the epileptic watch the television. Still no sound. Slow blues on the stereo now, a singer who's nearly screaming.

ONE HUNDRED THOUSAND DEAD.

The words cross the bottom of the screen.

"Holy shit," the epileptic says.

"Yeah," says his friend.

"How long you fuckers staying here?" the dipping man now says, his voice muddied by the pile of dip under his tongue.

And the carousel operator knows what's happening now. He's late to it. The epileptic, of course, he'd realized right away. But now the carousel operator is realizing. He's late to this. Because he's a lot of things. Things that are bad. But he's never once cared about the color of someone's skin.

The carousel operator is a thin kid. Not that tall. He doesn't shave.

He stands from his barstool now.

The man with the dip already loves this. "Is he your fucking boyfriend?" the man asks, an accusation as he points at the epileptic, voice still altered by the huge load of dip.

The epileptic turns from this man to his new friend, the carousel operator, ready to get out of here. Ready to walk away. Why bother? A scene repeated through his entire life. His dead brother's life. All his friends' lives. A story his mother told him as a child, that would repeat itself, over and again, and sometimes you fight and sometimes you walk, because if all you do is fight, his mother said, you'll fight your entire life, consumed finally with an anger that you can't let go of or control.

But as the epileptic turns to the operator of the carousel across from his own ride at the fair, he sees the kid now in this bar in the middle of the night and knows something different has already started.

The man with the dip wants to speak again. He's ready to posture. Hurl insults. Intimidate the two of them. But he can't. Because the kid from the carousel has already hit him in the mouth. The kid hits him again. And again. The kid keeps hitting him, even when the man is on the ground. Bloody. Eyes closed.

Lame hands held up.

Wait. Stop.

But the kid doesn't stop. Doesn't hesitate. He's down on one knee. Hitting the man repeatedly. Methodically. Like a doctor giving CPR. Or a butcher at work on a steer.

The man with the dip has friends, of course. Who stand. Three of them. Whether they know him or just sympathize, they are about to join the fight.

The kid turns to them and before any of them can step forward, the kid has grabbed one of them, a man, much bigger, he's fat, the kid pulls him forward, so that the fat man's momentum takes him to the ground as the kid knees him in the face, then steps around and begins to hit another of the friends, again and again, until he also falls.

The epileptic is still holding his beer. Watching. Stunned. He hasn't had a chance to understand this. All he knows is the condensation on his bottle. Dripping cold across his thumb.

But what he sees already is something he feels but can't yet say. What he feels is not this kid's ability or grace or some sort of preparation or training for the assault he's launched against these dumb hicks here in the bar. What the epileptic sees is a willingness.

The willingness to cause harm.

One of the friends of the man with the dip is the man who is missing an arm.

It's bad.

The carousel operator throws him to the ground, holding his one arm behind him, the epileptic watching as the kid twists that one arm so far that it separates from the shoulder or maybe it's broken. All the epileptic knows or anyone knows, any of these people who watch this fight under the dim lights of this warehouse now operating as a bar—the music's so loud with the drums and grinding guitar, and the singer has begun to moan, howling really, the man keeps howling—but all any of them know is the screaming, above the music now, the one-armed man can only scream.

The fat man gets on his feet. Grabs the kid. Holds him tight. Starts hitting him hard in the side of the head. Fist on skull. The kid's eyes close. His head shakes with every blow.

But the kid is able to grab the man's arm. He twists it. Badly. Till the man lets go of the kid, screaming, the kid pushing back on the man and they both fall to the floor.

But the kid, the carousel operator, his friend of these few hours, it's like the floor wakes him up; repelled by it, he's standing, and another of the dipping man's friends is on him.

And so the violence spreads.

This man carries scars as well, across the face. He's probably thirty, and he's big and strong and he'd walked forward slowly, having watched what's happening, smiling with disdain, knowing that he's stronger and tougher than anyone he's ever met in all his life.

What the kid does to him leaves everyone in the room in a self-imposed silence. The kid hits this man first in the nose, breaking it, a pain even the strong man can't but stop to feel. And stopping leaves him open to a circling violence, the kid hitting the man in his ear, the other ear; he swings once with his hand open, and he may well have punctured the man's left eye, there's blood and there's fluid and the man has dropped to the floor. But still the kid is circling. Slowly. Hitting him in the throat, in the side of the neck. He hits him again in the nose.

The man's strength, probably, works against him at this point. Because he stays partly upright. He doesn't curl up. He doesn't pass out. Or die.

The kid hits him again in the throat. There's something about this. How he hits him in the throat. The epileptic considers this. In the seconds that substitute for normal moments or minutes. This kid he barely knows embodies a violence he didn't recognize, has never known, that at most he read about in some classroom for literature or heard about on a street corner, the stories of legend and fear that no one challenged but that, still, no one ever in their hearts could truly, honestly believe.

Finally, the man lets himself lie down on the floor.

The kid is covered in blood. Both his hands. He's bleeding from his nose and mouth and the side of his head. There's blood down the front of his shirt, as if he's spilled a bowl of it on himself.

He turns, looks around, takes in the entire room.

After a moment of stillness, the kid kicks the first man in the face. The guy with the dip who pushed his black friend. A brown, fibrous wad now spills out across the wooden floor. It lies near the guy's bleeding mouth. The kid kicks him again. Again in the mouth.

The man's face now, it's misshapen. Warped.

His palette, the epileptic thinks. The kid's fucking broken the man's palette.

All this has taken just a few minutes. Not even five.

A violence beyond what anyone present can ever describe.

A violence unspeakable.

A violence that, clearly, is only a repetition of so many moments in this kid's life.

And on the television, the epileptic sees, turning now, as if the fight had not happened at all, he turns to see the buildings fall. Three of them. This is live. Happening now. One after another. Collapsing, disintegrating, gone, already washed over with the water that continues to flow.

• • •

Everyone can sing. It's not clear how. It's not clear why. No hymnals. No program. No common book or printed words of song or prayer. But when they sing, they find the tune, the note, the voice all mean to express. The singing rises, but in a sense, it's wordless. Really, these are only sounds.

The words are the least important of it all.

He'd prefer to avoid the desperation.

Settle terms. Exchange cash. Move on to why they stand together in this deserted playground.

He wishes he could afford a hotel.

He wishes he had a girlfriend.

He wishes he were long since married.

He wishes he even knew this woman's name.

But none of these things has, for him, ever once seemed possible.

CHAPTER 8
THE DOCTOR

Cities where the flu spreads like a plague.

Not the plague of olden times.

Not some virus wiping out humanity in all its forms.

Just the flu. That kills the elderly, small children, the undernourished, and the poor.

• • •

Still these two years later, his wife refuses to speak in English. Even though she's long spoken it better than him.

"Please," he says to her.

She shakes her head. Lying on her small bed. She won't eat today. He knows already that she won't. But he tries again.

"Please," he says.

"No," she says. She picks up her book. Reads again by the sunlight that illuminates the white canvas around them.

Someone knocks on the flimsy door frame to their tent. He goes from this room, where they live, to the next room. A room created simply by two sheets of canvas hung from the ceiling. But they call it a room.

The woman knocking has a prescription that needs updating. Medicine for her heart condition. The doctor renews the prescription he wrote for her.

The doctor is allowed to prescribe drugs still. And so he does. He's allowed to treat patients still. Even perform certain operations. And so he does those things too.

The authorities here, they welcome anyone who relieves them of a service they are required to supply.

And the doctor needs the money. To pay for a tent he and his wife can live in without other people. To purchase better food than the rations distributed twice a week from the back of a truck. To buy protection for himself and, especially, his wife.

Why wouldn't he want to buy these things?

He's been a doctor for more than ten years. Before coming here, they had a home with a courtyard. A bedroom that overlooked the bay.

The doctor cannot distribute the drugs. The security firm handles that. But they will honor his prescriptions.

And, of course, the doctor is paid in cash.

There are almost one hundred thousand people living in this camp. Just across the border. Built alongside the wall.

Building the camp here was a mistake. There are tunnels underneath the wall that come out in tents in the heart of the camp. It is not just the easy access between both countries that's a problem. It's the economics of the matter. People in the camp have many financial needs. Helping others cross the border is an easy source of money.

The people who come through a tunnel into a camp like this, they are mostly transporting drugs. The people who want freedom, who want to escape into the cities and farms to the north to start a life here, to work and live and marry, all of them now use boats, not land. Once the wall was finished, it blocked the easy overland entrances that had existed for so many decades.

That's when the migrants shifted to boats.

The number of migrants didn't change. All that changed was the number who died in crossing.

Sometimes refugees are able to buy their way out of the camp through these same tunnels. But the cost is now beyond the means of all but a very few.

He finishes writing prescriptions. Finishes with his patients. He's checked a man's sprained arm. He's checked a child's pink eye. He's checked a woman's belly.

Yes, he tells her, *you are pregnant*.

She begins to cry. He's not sure if they are tears of sadness. She hides her eyes, and so he isn't sure. But if she's sad, unbearably so, then she will be back. He does not need to tell her that he can take care of that issue too.

She leaves. He steps outside for a moment.

They have no children, the doctor and his wife. They could never conceive. Even with the help of drugs and doctors. There was no diagnosis. They tried every option. All failed.

They are forty now. They tried for fifteen years.

He wonders, of course, if he'd have been able to have children with a different woman.

For him, it's a merely clinical question.

His wife, he thinks, she wonders this too. But for her, he is sure, it's a different question. One unspoken. Never discussed.

He simply sees it in her eyes.

• • •

Hospitals have set up tents in their huge parking lots. Treating children and the elderly, all of whom have the flu. Some die. Most do not. Billions of dollars are spent treating the illness. Doctors turn to the TV cameras, begging everyone, next year, to please get vaccinated.

"This could be so much less severe," one doctor says, "if everyone listening simply got one shot."

• • •

He and his wife crossed the border knowing they'd likely end up in a camp like this. First, they walked a hundred miles through the desert to the coast. Then they paid their way onto a small boat. Once a fishing boat, it was

99

loaded now with almost fifty people. This was the safest boat they could afford. It was intercepted within a few days of being out in the Gulf. After much processing, days of questions, they were taken to this camp.

The doctor and his wife knew this could happen. But the violence at home had gotten to where they could no longer stay. Friends of theirs disappeared. Police demanded larger bribes for even less protection. Homes near theirs were firebombed in the night.

Drug violence. All of it. Violence institutionalized. Violence fueled unintentionally by the desperate flood of workers fleeing the thousands of failing farms and villages throughout the countryside.

They had known a camp like this was likely. But it was a theory then, a thing they'd read about, heard about, seen in videos and read about in the papers.

There are five of these camps. Spread evenly across the border. The biggest of them are on the coasts, camps that hold the migrants who can't escape the coast guard or the navy, or who can't escape the weather or the fragility of their small boats, or who can't escape the callus ineptitude of their sea captains or overland guides. The camps on the coasts hold many hundreds of thousands of migrants.

In that sense, the doctor and his wife are fortunate. This camp is smaller, less chaotic.

He's not sure why they were brought to this one.

Luck.

"Have you gone to the administrators today?" she asks. In Spanish, of course.

"Not yet," he says in English.

She turns back to what she's reading. He sits near her. Reading a newspaper.

In theory, the camps are only holding pens. Where the administrators tend to the migrants as they wait to be processed before release. Background checks. Medical screening. Citizenship tests. An assessment of one's reasons for seeking asylum.

What do you want? What will you do? Will you make something or only take?

In reality, far fewer are released than gain entry to the camps. The politics, the economy, the fear engendered by stories of crime and violence. All combine to keep the doctor and his wife and the hundred thousand people around them detained here indefinitely.

He takes a sip of wine. Offers his wife a glass. She declines. Lunch was chicken and rice with fresh tomatoes grown in the camp. The girl who cooks for them worked for years in one of the luxury hotels on the Gulf's coast, back before the hotels began to close.

Beaches steadily washed away. Hillside resorts that no amount of rocks or concrete barriers could keep from collapsing into the ocean. Heat that fewer and fewer travelers chose to bear.

Some days, he knows, he's come to find a comfort in how he lives here. In his position, his authority over his patients. His relationship with the authorities.

He never mentions this to his wife. She'd kill him, probably. If she even knew such a thought had crossed his mind. She'd slit his throat in the middle of the night.

Not an idle thought.

She's the daughter of a drug lord. He ruled the southern provinces. Until he, like all of them are eventually, was taken away in the night. Stripped. Tortured. Slowly killed. By another drug lord, one who wished very much to replace him.

One who would later be taken away in the night himself.

That the daughter, his wife, was only thrown out to live in the street is hard to believe. Just fourteen. Most like her, the fallen families of drug lords deposed, are raped, and tortured, and eventually also killed.

She was allowed to leave. For years she lived abroad, she told him. On her own. He met her when she was twenty-five.

He looks at her on her small bed. Eyes closed. Dark hair across her pillow. A beautiful woman. Pretending to sleep.

But she is only thinking. Waiting. Wanting to leave this horrific place.

• • •

"And you know," she says, on television, a doctor, calm but her exasperation shows at the edges of every sentence, "you need to know, nothing will kill more people this year than obesity, inactivity, and the simple, stupid choices people make."

• • •

In the night, he wakes as she gets into bed with him. Whispering in Spanish, touching him, she has him ready before he's even really awake, atop him, moving gently. She whispers still, between her short breaths. He's half asleep, half awake, she kisses his neck and then his chest, pushing harder. But almost silent. She comes soon, probably she'd been touching herself in her bed before this started. Her breasts just barely brush against his chest as she rocks forward, back again, whispering to him, and he comes now too.

She'll sleep the rest of the night with him.

He loves her. The way she touches him. The way she smells.

He hates so much the many ways in which he's failed.

In the morning, he sees patients in the front room of their tent. They're lined up to see him. He has a nurse who works with him. She was a scrub nurse working on transplants at one of the university hospitals. She is much overqualified for the job. The colds people have. The pains and vague discomfort.

Most of the illnesses here are a function of the sadness people feel. The worry that they won't ever get out of this camp. The depression that this is all their journey will possibly achieve.

This is his worry too. So few visas are now issued. So many more people cross the border, most caught and sent directly to these camps. Fear of the refugees grows steadily. Anger toward them. Resentment and distrust, and for many people it is simple hatred.

His cousin made it out of his camp. Legally. He lives far west now, in a city there. He tells the doctor about the hatred. He's an architect working as a cab driver and weekend busboy. Unable to get any other job despite the visa and work permit he was granted many years ago. "They don't like us," the doctor's cousin says when they speak by phone. "They see us all in the same light. We've come here to take, they think. Take money. Take jobs. Offer nothing. Give nothing. I tell people I designed office buildings. Hospitals. A library. A museum. They look at me and laugh."

Some part of the doctor wonders if they're not better off here. In this camp.

He knows this is wrong. He shuts down the thought. He thinks again that were his wife to hear him say such a thing, were she to know he'd ever thought this, she would be uncontained.

He checks patients' eyes. He listens to their lungs. He listens to their heartbeats. He looks over each of them for signs of any of the truly terrible diseases that could sweep across this camp. Cholera or dysentery. Measles. Some sort of flu.

He's paid in cash. There's a price list. Some people can't afford it. He takes what they can offer.

Most everyone offers something.

With the money they give him, he can buy extra supplies. Medicines beyond the allotment that the authorities who run this place give to him and the other doctors.

Coldhearted, often violent, the men and women of the security firm officially in charge of this camp spend most of their time patrolling the high fence bordering this camp. They monitor the occupants with binoculars, with drones that buzz overhead around the clock. Periodically, they'll drive through the camp in a long train of black SUVs.

If security enters this place on foot, it is only in force, a group of forty of them in their dark uniforms, heavy helmets. They come in to arrest some former member of the drug trade or a gang.

However, some of the security guards enter the camps late at night. Headed to the brothels. They're given deep discounts. The best girls. New ones. Fresh.

The doctor treats the prostitutes. For ailments professional and otherwise. He treats them in his office sometimes. But he also goes to them during the day, where they live. Some doctors won't. But he will. Like the children who come to him without parents or family, the prostitutes he treats without charging them anything at all.

...

"There's so little I can do," she says, on the television. "I'm a doctor to bodies. Not minds. And what most people have, what they are experiencing as pain, is a symptom of choices and illnesses that originate in their minds. Real illnesses, not imagined. But not ones I can ever possibly solve."

...

The security firm assures that the refugees are contained in the camp. But the camp itself was long ago taken over by the members of a gang. Extensions of the cartel, the various gangs almost immediately sent members to run the camps across the border.

In many ways, though, the camps are more peaceful than the cities people fled. In the cities south of here, the gangs are at war over territory, shipping routes, shrinking cropland, limited water, labor to process the crops and drugs. But across the border, each camp is dominated by just one gang. By agreement, the gangs have split these places among themselves. Thus, there are no turf wars. No disputes that go unsettled.

There's a hierarchy to the gang's control over the camp. Representatives from each area of the camp sit on a council that brings issues to the leadership. The council determines the fair distribution of water, food, and medicine and is especially concerned with the safety of families, women, and children. The gang tolerates no petty crime, no theft or fighting. Gambling is controlled and limited to specific tents in the camp. Alcohol and drugs are available, but open abuse is not allowed. The gang's tax rates are quite reasonable, less than what most people paid to the corrupt governments they left behind.

Some in the camps consider the gangs to be, at worst, benign. Still others view the gangs as the saviors of all these unwanted refugees.

The doctor might think so too. Were it not for the women they keep in the very busy brothels.

And the drugs and guns they transport across the border through the tunnels.

And the young girls they traffic north, every week, through those same passageways.

The doctor treats these girls as they are moved through the camp. Before they are transported north. Human packages, often sold by their parents or deceived into this choice with promises of jobs, visas, the freedom and safety of places to the north. Promises of relief from the hopelessness, the misery, the endless sorrow in which they lived back home.

The doctor goes twice a week to the tents that hold these girls. The food for the girls is better. The tents clean and stocked with fresh clothes and bedding. The gangs make available any and all medicines the doctor might need. He checks the girls for disease. He gives them full batteries of tests, completes their vaccinations. He administers birth control, simple implants in their arms. That is required for them all.

Some girls he sterilizes. A choice the gang lets the girls make on their own.

The doctor sometimes feels he is only prepping these girls to be more efficiently abused. To assure the survival of these high-priced investments as they head north for a life of rape and torture. He's a veterinarian to prized cattle, maximizing their health before they're sent to a long and conscious slaughter.

He pauses for a moment. Closes his eyes. After a minute, he pats the dark-haired girl on her slim shoulder. She smiles some. He smiles back.

As he leaves the tent, the gang member at the door offers him money. As always, the doctor says no thank you.

He walks back toward his tent. It is nearly a mile from one end of the camp to the other. It is hot today. And still. Probably more than one hundred and twenty degrees. In the two years he's been in this camp, he's treated hundreds, maybe a thousand, of the girls who are trafficked north. He declines the gang's money. But the gang does treat him well. He has access to more medicine. He is given better food. His wife is safe. He is too.

A bargain he made without wanting to be part of it.

A thousand girls. Made healthier than they've ever been. Made infertile for a time. Or for their whole lives. Made ready for the work they'll do.

Made ready by him.

They are shuttled through tunnels that head north, under the camp fence, emptying in fields near highways far from here. Met by buses that continue their transport.

For some of them, he's sure, his is the last kind face they'll ever know.

• • •

"Honestly?" she repeats, looking down for a moment. Pondering the question. "Well," she says, looking up now, "honestly, I often leave my office feeling hopeless. That's how I feel. That's my answer to your question. Hopeless. I go to the clinic. I see patients. I prescribe drugs when that is best. But more and more often, I prescribe exercise, a change of lifestyle. *'Get outside,'* I'll write neatly on my small and stupid notepad. *'Take a walk with family and friends.'* Then later, after I've left these patients to dress and leave, I'll return to the room they occupied. And I'll see that the prescriptions I have written are simply crumpled up and left behind."

By day he works among the lifeless bodies in the basement. He adorns their faces with rouge and lipstick. Dresses their upper bodies in clothing of his recommendation and the family's choice.

He does this day after day.

There was a time when the act would have been profound.

Now, though, it's become just another routine.

CHAPTER 9
THE RESTAURANT MANAGER

Money made off the creation of life-saving medications.

Money made off an understanding of institutional requirements so complex they can barely be deciphered.

Money made in honor of the deaths of fallen soldiers.

Money made off children. The elderly. The brilliant. The unreal.

Sometimes, he says, *it's as if we linger in the world of the undead.*

His cousin stares at him. *Fuck you,* he says. Not smiling. *Fuck you totally.*

• • •

The wind here blows hard. A dry, hot wind, coming from the west, sweeping down off the mountains and gusting thirty to forty miles an hour all day. It pushes hard enough that it sometimes shoves the trucks and cars three and four feet across the painted lines on the highway. It strips loose shingles from all the homes. It has rendered two runways at the airport unusable. It shapes the landscape, bending shrubs and trees and flowers, all arcing, bowed, their tops curling over, leaning far to the east.

It's been this way for years. Every day. The wind does not relent.

It rains today, suddenly, but it won't last long. It doesn't rain much here, and when it does come, it's always a short, near-violent outburst of a storm, the dark clouds rolling down from the mountains, pushed hard by the constant wind, so that a front of rain pouring sideways assaults the city. It hits the airport first, shutting down the one runway that can still be used. It hits the stadium next, that glass and steel wonder with the view of the mountains to the west. The wind already makes it a miserable place, but with the rainstorm, people must flee their seats. The rain then hits the highway, a barely winding ribbon drawn north to south, vehicles driving parallel to the wind and now the water pours sideways, shaking cars and trucks, and in the fray of the storm many cars pull over to the shoulder of the highway, hundreds of cars now parked on a freeway meant to link this city to all the world.

Every few weeks a vehicle on the highway will begin to bounce, the car soon rocking side to side, and the driver will lose control, the car veering into the other lane and then onto the shoulder and eventually the car is blown from the highway, careening into the sunken dirt median.

There was an eighty-car pileup here less than a year ago. A chain reaction of interrelated wrecks, all starting with a car that was blown hard enough to finally bounce off of a guardrail.

There was a fifty-car pileup a year before that.

A thirty-car pileup a year before that.

The western side of the city is slowly fading into the same washed-out lack of color. The wind, combined with the dirt and dust from the plains beyond the highway, is methodically wearing down the western-facing surfaces of buildings and homes and plant life. Painted structures fading to a dull and weathered tan. Tree bark turning pale. Glass has lost its shine. Billboards that face west are quickly stripped of their printed surfaces; instead all of them now carry the distant, ghostlike images of people and places and slogans long since worn away.

He is watching a documentary on a news channel. About the city north of here that was, years ago, eventually abandoned. He's eating dinner. Reading on his phone. Glancing up at the documentary only intermittently.

The wind rattles the windows on one side of his house, as if an animal were clawing at the glass.

He glances at the plastic plants in his living room and small dining room. His mother's once, now his.

He'll masturbate later. Eat ice cream before that. Do budget work on his laptop. Read a book. Then sleep.

He is manager of a chain of hamburger restaurants. A national chain. He runs the five stores they have in this small city. Some nights, he meets his girlfriend for dinner. They don't have sex yet; she wants to wait, and he's said that's fine.

It is fine. He's thirty. He's had sex. Girlfriends who wanted that right away. It can wait.

He knows it will be better if they wait.

She texts him a photo while he sits working at his kitchen table. She's in a pajama top. Nothing else. The top not fully buttoned. Her way of saying good night.

He texts her back. She's very pretty.

You are very pretty.

He turns on the game he's been waiting to watch. He's been recording it on his cable box, then waiting half an hour to start watching. This way he can skip the commercial breaks. Plus, the game doesn't take as long. Friends will sometimes text him about a good play, a bad call, and he has to be careful not to read their messages, because the texts might give away the score or tell him what is about to happen.

Time just slightly altered. For efficiency and convenience. He knows other people who watch games this way.

In bed later, after the game, he'll get his phone out. Bring up the picture his girlfriend sent. Others she's texted recently. He moves through them with his thumb. It's just a minute or two before he comes.

• • •

We make money illegally, the CEO tells his cousin. *What we sell will eventually break. We know this. That's illegal.*

His cousin is his partner. The CEO watches him shake his head.

No, his cousin says. *We make money unethically.* He takes a drink. *There's a difference.*

• • •

110

Most of the people working for him in the kitchens have come here illegally. The others have criminal records that they've tried to hide. He doesn't care. If they work hard. If they show up on time. If they don't bring trouble.

Then they're not criminals to him.

A third of them are white. A third black. A third from below the border.

He doesn't plan for this. It's just always so.

"Quickly, people," he says, smiling some, moving between the two sets of grills, "quickly."

He's a tall man, fit. Black hair and olive skin. He eventually wants to open his own restaurant. But for now, he's still learning. What it takes to manage cash flow. Hire well. Deal with suppliers. Sell specials to new customers.

There's plenty of time to start his own place.

"Lunch hour soon," he says to his people running the cash registers, women mostly. Some still adjust their uniforms, just off the bus or out of their mother's car. "Offer the upgrades. Every order, please. Every order includes an offer to add an item. Yes? Please?"

The front door crashes open, slamming against the outer glass wall. A customer stumbles, thrown off balance. The manager trots across the restaurant. Checking on the woman and her son.

"The wind," the woman says. "Damn it. Damn wind."

He helps her inside. Tells her son he can get a free ice cream. *Sorry.* The trouble with the door. He's sorry.

She smiles. The boy smiles brightly. They move to the counter to order.

He's had to convince the regional manager to move the entrances of some of the other restaurants from one side of the building to the other. The wind is that strong. People could not open or close the door. And those who did, sometimes the door would be shoved open so quickly, so hard, that the customers would be knocked down.

Tonight, on his laptop, he'll put in a recommendation to move this door as well. Already the emergency exit from the restaurant is pinned shut. The wind makes opening that door impossible.

Now, he walks out into the parking lot.

The two-story building next door to this restaurant is under construction. Someone recently tore down the old building that had been there. Which changed the landscape. Allowing the wind to hit the front door of this restaurant more directly than before.

The wind is dry and hot, and he looks to the west. The bits of dirt and sand in the air sting his face. He squints his eyes.

He's not from here. He moved here for the job.

Where he lived, there was constant rain.

The plastic plants in his house, he's never much thought about them.

His mother had them. Now he does too.

• • •

His cousin walks to the table near the window. Puts his drink down. Looks out across the city. Lit bright at night, avenues leading north and south, streets to the east and west, cars moving in a red yellow glow, like cells in an artery or vein.

I fucking hate when you talk this way, his cousin says. *Like I'm a fucking criminal.*

You're not a criminal, the CEO says, now staring up at the high ceiling. It's the middle of the night. Here in his office. His apartment is one floor above. Often, it seems he has chosen to live among the clouds.

There's a woman there. Waiting for him.

You're not the criminal, the CEO says again to his cousin. He takes a drink, gin, there's a vapor to it, rising from his mouth, through and across his nose; it just barely waters his eyes. *We both are.*

• • •

He wakes up early. Goes to the gym to exercise. Lifting weights. Running on a treadmill. He's at the restaurant, the one downtown, near Fifty-Third Street, as the crew is opening for the day. He meets with each employee. But only for a minute.

They have work to do. He knows this. Empty platitudes are not necessary.

He just tells them how good a job they do.

· · ·

What we do is allowed, his cousin says. *Why can't you see that?*

The CEO sips again from the gin. The woman upstairs, she'll wait for him. He knows that. He can take as long as he wants. He says to his cousin, *I wish we'd never started this.*

His cousin shakes his head. *You're the only person I've ever loved,* he says. *Ever cared for. Who ever cared for me.*

They both look out at the city. There's a scope to the city that they can't comprehend. The colors. The sound. Too many people to contemplate. More than anyone can ever catalog. Or quantify. Or relay.

This, the CEO says to his cousin, *has nothing to do with love.*

· · ·

He wants very much to live a life of some substance. He can't define it. This thing he wants.

But he knows clearly what he feels.

· · ·

Below them, by day, five thousand people work for the two of them. They flood in from the city. Rising from subways and emerging from cabs and they make their way down these avenues. Coming here for the promise. A promise they've been made. That the work they do has meaning. That they themselves have purpose. That they work here not just for a salary. They work here because what they do might change the world.

It's just a fucking business, his cousin says.

The CEO shakes his head. *It's not,* he says.

His cousin shrugs. *Tell me we're still family.*

He doesn't hesitate. *We are.*

Then that's all I care about.

The CEO closes his eyes. They live a lie. A lie he can't find a way to unwind. So they continue. They work. People devote themselves. To a company. A job. Finding meaning in a place that's empty at its core.

We're not alone in doing this, his cousin says. *People, everywhere, do this all the time.*

The CEO drinks again. He'll go upstairs. Find escape in his dark and secret habit. She's paid to wait. If he wants, she can wait all night.

Probably, she'd prefer that.

He opens his eyes. Looks at his cousin. He has no idea how this will end.

CHAPTER 10

THE CAROUSEL OPERATOR

There is one woman; he met her at a church service. A service he had to attend. His mother insisted.

The woman he met there, daughter of his mother's friend, they talked afterward. And they laughed.

She's wounded, clearly. A wounded person.

He does not know why.

But now she comes to his small apartment. Once or twice a week. They hold each other. They both cry quietly. There's more to this than either of them can admit.

Afterward, while she dresses in the bathroom, he leaves money near her purse.

Which she takes.

They never talk about it. But when she's gone, the money is no longer there.

CHAPTER 10
THE CAROUSEL OPERATOR

In fact, crime has fallen. Fewer murders, fewer robberies; rapes are down, assaults decline.

But it does not feel that way.

Fewer cars are stolen. Fewer people harmed.

But to watch the television, to read the newspaper is to be told you are in danger. *At any moment, you, your family, anyone and everyone you have ever known, all of you are in danger.*

• • •

The two of them walk along the rural road leading back to the parking lot carnival.

The epileptic has been whistling. A soft tune, passage from a hymn. He whistles it again and again.

The carousel operator is mostly breathing. Quietly. Evenly. They both recognize in their separate ways that the most important thing is for him to breathe. It's been this way for the twenty minutes since they left the bar. Maybe it's been thirty.

No one has spoken.

It's dark except for the stars above them.

The first thing they say comes from the epileptic. "What a horrible way to die," he says. "Sitting in your car. Water. Three or four feet high."

The carousel operator begins to nod.

"And those buildings that fell," the epileptic says. "Consider the horror such a catastrophe entails."

The carousel operator glances at him as he walks. Then nods.

They walk another long while in silence. The silence of not speaking, at least. Because, against the backdrop of this abandoned rural landscape, the two of them are very loud. Their shoes hit the asphalt. The epileptic and his light whistling. The carousel operator, periodically, he slowly rubs his hands across his chest. His neck and arms. The palm of his hand against his skin makes a sound like sandpaper on a board.

The kid is checking, it seems, that all of his body is still there. And unharmed.

"I've been in fights," the epileptic says. "Kicked some ass. Had my ass kicked."

They walk. Another while. When they hear a vehicle approaching from behind, they both step down into the gully along the road. Squat. Lean back. Hidden. An immediate, unspoken agreement.

The car passes. They climb up to the road. Walking again.

The carousel operator says quietly, "I told you." When he speaks, he's not sure it's loud enough to be heard.

They walk awhile.

"You did," the epileptic says. "But I didn't know."

In a few minutes, the carousel operator nods. "Yeah."

"What's it feel like?" the epileptic asks now, immediately. He has the long, dead branch of a tree in his hands. He picks the atrophied needles from the bark. Releases them into the air.

"I can't say," his friend says.

The epileptic nods.

The road bends and, ahead of them, half a mile away, they see the bright white glow of the shopping center. Lit like daylight all the time. The silhouettes of the carnival rides stand barely noticeable near the outer darkness of the parking lot.

"Fucking home," the epileptic says.

"Like I control death," his friend says. "Like I determine outcomes I had no part in starting."

The epileptic releases his needles. There's not much of a wind, but what's there catches the needles, holds them; they reflect shallow bits of moonlight in the sky. "That's like God," says the epileptic.

Their feet tap, almost lightly, against the black-topped surface of this road.

The carousel operator closes his eyes. He walks without thinking about where he's going.

"I guess," the kid says. "Yes." He sees his steps. "But it's still not something I've ever wanted to feel."

• • •

Tell the rape victim that crime is down. Tell the dead boy's mother that crime is down. Tell the man whose house was emptied while he simply went to church. Tell the woman without insurance whose car is forever gone.

Tell them crime is down. And see how they respond.

• • •

In the morning, their last morning at the shopping center, the carousel operator works his ride. It's a weekday, Wednesday, he thinks, so the crowd is very light.

Parents, sometimes their kids, stare at the dark bruises on the side of his head.

He just nods. Averts his eyes.

He doesn't know where the carnival will go next. He assumes that he could ask. But, really, he doesn't care. Like the phones for sale in the dollar stores near their parking lots. He sees them. They are cheap. But who does he have to call? What news or show or information would he use that phone to see?

He's left the place where he grew up. He won't go back. Not ever. That is all there is.

The carousel winds down. The music seeming to get louder as the carousel slows. But it's only the lack of motion, gears no longer whining, the engine that drives this ride beginning to idle almost quietly.

Like he's supposed to, the carousel operator now yells, "Next!"

He hates this job.

Back home there were his friends. Three of them. Together they were four. Roaming that city. Walking and running through the woods that divided the pale neighborhoods where they lived. In cars driving faster than possible along a waterfront that glowed with ships and a pulp mill and the constant, controlled flames from the oil processing plant.

Back home he and his friends were gods.

A reputation earned through violence of all kinds. Worse than can be spoken. Too much for him to say. Bodies they beat bloody, meat, not human, the four of them inflicting pain on some tall motherfucker who challenged just one of them.

He takes tickets. With his right hand. Then transfers them to his left.

His fingers ache. All of them swollen.

There were girls then. A city where violence and the aura of power could gain favors with girls wanting their own escape.

He starts up the ride.

Horrors unspoken. Only lived.

Yet now he'll sometimes see his life back there for what it was. Now he wakes, in the night, in his tent on the edge of the light from a shopping center, and he wonders how he's alive.

The carousel blurs in front of him as he holds his head so still.

And there was a girl, of course. One girl that he now thinks about.

He thinks about her most every day.

He needs to hit the stop button on the carousel. He's late to punch it. He can see the timer. The kids, though, the parents who ride with them, he knows that they'll be pleased. Extra time.

The carousel blurs again.

Of course, there was a girl.

Watch a shooting scene caught on camera.

See a murder in the street.

Have your sibling describe the feeling of being carjacked in her driveway.

Even if all of it was done by someone that each victim once called a friend.

• • •

The epileptic talks, almost to himself. "Some places I can go and no one gives a shit about my color," he says.

They're sitting on the back of a flatbed truck. Tucked in between the metal arms of the brightly painted teacup ride, now folded up like a kid's pop-up book left high up on a shelf.

"It'll be this way for days," the epileptic says. "Weeks. Long enough that I almost forget about the racists."

The carousel operator stares backward, down the highway they've been traveling.

The air is hot enough that, like others working for the carnival, he and the epileptic decided to ride outside, in the wind on the back of the trucks. Cooler than the overloaded cabs of the company vans.

"And then," says the epileptic, "some fucker will want to call me a nigger."

His friend listens. Staring backward. It's ten in the morning. The sun burns hot.

The epileptic says, "There are a lot of ways to call me a nigger."

The kid nods some. "I don't say that word."

The epileptic nods.

In a minute, the carousel operator says, "My father told me not to."

The epileptic asks, "You break your hand in that fight?"

The carousel operator looks down, at his hands resting on his knees. His jeans. "I can't really move the right one," he says. "I could yesterday. But not now."

120

The epileptic nods slowly. "Motherfucking badass fight," he says.

His friend looks away. Along the highway, the trees are brown. As if burned by a fire that swept through here weeks ago. The carousel operator says, "I would rather not ever get in a fight again."

The epileptic nods. "Badass fight."

His friend nods.

"I mean," the epileptic says. Pauses. Wipes his dark hands across his pants. The pants were white once. But they're now tan with a filth the carousel operator shares. "I mean," the epileptic says, but then stops again. "Why do you fight like that?"

The kid, his friend, takes a minute. "My friends," he says.

The epileptic nods. "Three friends, you said before. Right?"

The kid nods.

"You just about killed that man," the epileptic says to him. "You know that, right?"

The kid remembers others who lay bloody on the ground. The kid remembers cars moving so fast that the motion of it was all you could understand. Or know. Or feel. The kid remembers crossing along undeveloped high ridges, woods near their homes, where no one ever went. Except him and his friends.

The carousel operator finally answers. "I know that."

The epileptic nods. "Then at least the two of us know that much."

The kid turns slightly toward him. Smiles some.

It's not a warm smile. But it's the best that he can do.

"I've seen bad things," the epileptic says. "I've seen abuse. But, man," he says, turning fully toward his friend, "I've never seen anything like what you did to those men."

"Like I said," the friend says, closing his eyes, warm air getting hotter, pushing across his face and his swollen hands and pushing up through his jeans, "I'd rather not ever get in a fight again."

• • •

121

We're told the danger is right nearby. We're told to prepare for scenarios once unimaginable.

But the real dangers are already in our homes.

Your sister's drug-dealing boyfriend is the danger. Not a stranger on a street corner. Not a black man in a forgotten alley.

Your babysitting aunt with an addiction to alcohol and a history of being beaten by her own father, she is the real danger. Not the neighbor girl who takes care of the kids on the weekend. Not the college kid in need of cash, who responded to an ad online.

Your brother-in-law with the secret fetish for child porn is the danger. Not a stranger near the playground. Not that man shopping alone in aisle thirteen of the store.

• • •

In the new town, they spend the night and the morning setting up the carnival. Again in the parking lot of a big shopping center near the highway.

The carousel operator has learned how to set up his ride on his own. When the guy in charge comes by, he only has to nod.

It's morning. They won't open till four or five.

He leans against the metal rail bordering the teacup ride, standing in the shade created by the roof of the carousel. The epileptic stands near him, arms up, head leaned back, closing his eyes.

"Yoga," the epileptic says. "I taught it to myself."

The carousel operator nods.

"What else can you do?" the epileptic asks. "Besides fight."

There's a wind here. Constant. They'd thought it was just the wind from the drive. Or a wind in the morning. But they've been here since last night. And the wind has not relented.

The carousel operator shrugs. "Nothing. I've always worked. But I don't have a skill."

The epileptic nods. "I can't drive a car. I can't ride a bike. I don't even know how to swim." He turns to his friend. "Isn't that fucked?"

122

The carousel operator nods.

The epileptic asks, "How's the hand?"

His friend holds his hand up. He moves a few of the fingers. "These two are probably broken."

"I wish," the epileptic says, "for your sake, I wish that I could promise you there'd never be another fight."

His friend steps forward, into the sunlight. He turns his face up to the bright sky. Eyes closed. "I know," the kid says.

"What's the worst thing you've ever done?" the epileptic asks.

It's a long time before the kid answers. "Fights," he says. "Me and my friends. We would get in fights."

The heat in the sunlight is searing. But the wind blows. Hard. So it keeps him from sweating in the sun.

"And what's the worst thing that's ever happened to you?" the epileptic asks.

The kid doesn't hesitate. "Having to leave my friends behind."

• • •

One rape is too many.

One murder is too many.

One assault, one robbery, one car theft is too many.

Yet one will happen. In the next minute.

One just happened. A few moments ago.

For years, he went to church. Then stopped, when he could make that decision for himself.

But still, every Sunday, some part of him attends.

He does little on Sunday mornings. He likes to be alone throughout the day. On Sundays, he keeps away from televisions, computers, even phones. His mind walks through the motions of the service. The routines. The silences and shared declarations.

He reads from his books about religions.

On Sundays, alone in his apartment, he'll find himself quietly singing a hymn.

CHAPTER II
THE DOCTOR

Photos taken every moment of every day. Photos as language. A dialect. A method of communicating mood and location, desire and status. Photos taken together, huddled together, two people smiling emptily, two people smiling happily, two people not smiling, barely tolerating, but now is when you take a picture.

• • •

He is woken in the night. Men outside their tent. Pounding loudly on the thin door frame.

The doctor sits up. Confused. His wife is awake already. Standing naked between their beds, a knife held in her hand.

"If they were coming for us," he says, "they would not use the door."

She doesn't acknowledge him.

He stands. Pulls on pants and a shirt. Goes to the door.

Two members of the gang. Young ones. Teenage boys. They want him to come to another tent. A brother of theirs has been hurt.

He goes back inside to find shoes. A small backpack with medical supplies.

His wife still stands between their beds. Holding that knife in her hand.

He touches her, on the arm first, then holds her shoulders lightly. "It's all right," he whispers. "It's all fine."

125

In a dimly lit tent near the very middle of the camp, the doctor finds another teenager. Lying on a cot. He bleeds from many places. His side, his leg, multiple places on his arm.

The teenager is wrapped in sheets turned nearly black with blood. His face and hair are filthy dirty. His hands are too, covered in dirt and mud. He breathes quickly. His eyes are wide. But he can say nothing.

"He needs to go to the hospital," the doctor says to the two young gang members who have brought him here. The doctor hasn't even stepped forward. "He needs surgery. The hospital tent. He needs more help than I can give him here."

The two teenagers look at each other. They shake their heads. *No.*

The doctor looks at them. "He's going to die without a hospital," the doctor says.

The kid on the bed, bleeding and shaking, says in Spanish, "No hospital."

The other two shake their heads again. *No.*

It's hard to know what the three of them have been doing. But it's clear they've somehow been working on the side. In the tunnels, he assumes. Given how dirty the kid is. Running drugs or guns through the passageways. Or communicating, maybe, with a rival gang from another camp. Maybe trying to move a girl north. Or some family member.

The doctor doesn't know. But it's better that he doesn't. Whether their intent was evil or wise or benevolent or benign, he is only here to help.

The floor under the bed is thick with blood. The doctor checks each wound. Bullet holes. He can't possibly do anything to help the boy here. He simply gets fresh sheets. Presses them hard against each wound. Wraps other sheets tightly around the makeshift bandages.

He gets a syringe from his bag. Gives the boy a shot of painkiller. Soon the shaking stops. The boy slowly begins to nod.

The doctor stands watching him. There's nothing he can do.

"Can we have another of those?" one of the boys asks. Pointing at the syringe.

The doctor turns to him. "What are your names?" he asks in Spanish.

The boys don't hesitate to tell him.

"They will kill you all," the doctor says. "For whatever it is that you are doing. You can't outsmart them. You can't cheat them. You can't ever get away from them."

The boys nod.

"Where are you from?" he asks.

They tell him. A town not far from where he grew up.

"Make a new choice," the doctor says to the standing boys. "Or end up like your friend."

They nod.

From his bag, the doctor pulls out three vials. He hands them to one of the boys. "When he starts shaking again," the doctor says, "give him one of these. Okay?"

The boy nods.

"What is his name?" the doctor asks, turning back to the boy on the bed.

They tell him.

The boy, bleeding, blinks his eyes. Stares vaguely toward the doctor.

Moments later, the doctor turns to leave. But pauses. Closes his eyes. He doesn't turn back. Instead he says aloud, "The vials. The medicine. It is very strong. If you aren't careful," he hears himself say, "and you give him all of it at once, he'll die quickly. Quietly. Before you or he realize what has happened."

Outside, there is only the sliver of a moon in the sky. More stars than he ever remembers seeing. His town was near a city. Then he lived with his wife in another city.

Cities that washed all these stars from the sky.

Here, though, in this camp and across the miles of land around it, there is so little light. And so the night sky shines so brightly down on him. For a few minutes, he tries to count the stars. For a few minutes, he tries to fix the constellations long sought or barely witnessed.

But he can't.

Back at his tent, his wife sits in bed. Lamp on. Reading. He tells her about the wounded boy.

He notices her knife sits close to her, on the wooden crates they've turned into her bedside table.

"What did you do for him?" she asks.

He shrugs. Turns his hands up. Starts to answer but he can't. He needs a minute.

He says finally, "I told his friends how to help him die."

. . .

Photos that were originally taken on film. Photos more than a hundred years old, of cityscapes during the day. Horses pulling wooden carts. Women walking their children to school.

A longing to document daily life as it once was.

. . .

One of the girls being trafficked north thinks that she is pregnant.

"Why do you think this?" he asks her.

She tells him how long it's been since she had her period. He goes to the cabinet of medical supplies. Unlocks it and gets a pregnancy test for her. He hands it to the girl.

He goes outside while she's in the small, wooden bathroom. He squints as he stares up toward the sun. Hot and still and blinding. It's been months since they've had rain.

Ten minutes later, the girl returns. Holding the plastic device. She nods. He takes the test from her. Looks at it. He nods also.

She sits down on her bed. Looks away from him. Like all the girls, she wears just a white dress. She has long hair, dark, and light brown skin and she is beautiful in a specific way. Recognized but not described. Yet she looks like all the girls.

It's a part of this gang's brand.

The doctor gets a chair from nearby. Brings it to her bed. Sits. Staring at her.

The girl still looks away.

The doctor knows that normally the girls who pass through the camp have not yet been put to work. The gangs won't risk disease or pregnancy before the girls have been sold into service north of here. And so, the doctor wonders how this girl got pregnant. He wonders if the rules have changed. Or if she was working on her own, unbeknownst to the gang.

She turns to look at him. She is maybe fifteen. "What will happen if I have this baby?" she asks him. In English now. So that the guards outside the tent won't understand. Perfect English. The type taught in the private schools back in the south. "What will they do?"

The doctor stares at her. It's a moment before he answers. "They won't let you," he tells her finally. "Once you begin to show, they will make the decision for you."

She looks down at her hands.

"I loved that boy," she says. Still staring down at her hands.

"Who?" the doctor asks.

She looks up at him. "The boy," she says. Glancing down. Toward her belly. Looks at the doctor and says again, "The boy I loved."

It's a moment, then the doctor nods. In his mind, he chastises himself. For his assumptions. His callousness. Why wouldn't it be a boy? Why couldn't this girl be in love? Why couldn't she be a teenager who, swept up in a moment, simply was not careful?

"I'm sorry," he says out loud.

She nods. "Will you do the operation?" she asks. "Or will it be someone else?"

The question startles him. He's not sure why. It takes a moment to answer. "It's early enough that you don't need an operation," he says finally, "You will take a pill. Then there's another step. Simple. You'll take care of that yourself. This will take a few days. There will be a bit of blood. And cramping. But you'll be here the entire time."

She nods. "You'll give this pill to me?"

He stares. Usually his nurse does this. But he answers the girl. "Yes," he says. "I will give this pill to you."

She nods, again looking down. "There was a time when I had great hope for my life," she says.

He does not have anything to say.

She thanks him. He can only nod.

In a moment, as he still stands there, she looks up at him and says, "We will do it now."

The doctor gets the pill for her from the dispensary. He is supposed to tell the gang when any of the girls are pregnant. But he doesn't. The same if they have any disease.

He decided early on that the gang does not need to know.

Probably, he sometimes thinks, the gangs prefer this too.

He returns to the girl sitting on her bed. He holds the pill out to her. She closes her eyes, muttering something, then leans forward, her mouth open.

It's a moment before he realizes she expects him to put it on her tongue.

Finally, he does. Then holds the cup of water as she drinks from it. Carefully swallows.

After a moment, she thanks him one more time.

He shakes his head. *No need,* he whispers, in Spanish, but probably she can't hear him as she lies back down, turning away from him as she curls her knees up, slowly wrapping them in her arms.

Then the doctor moves on to the next girl on this row.

• • •

More photos than can ever really be viewed. Hundreds from just a night out with friends. A thousand from just one trip to the beach.

Revealing, mundane, staged, or blurry.

Moments not captured but created. An intrusion, artifice, photos retaken, again, until they're deemed to express some sort of perfection.

• • •

In the early morning, he makes love to his wife. She cries some, but smiles. *It's okay. Just sadness. But not sadness about you.*

New visas will be announced today. The end of the month. The reason for her crying.

She kisses him. Holds him close.

Later, he goes to the announcement. Held near the main entrance. Dutiful. He stands near the back of the crowd as names are read out by a man in a khaki suit standing on the bed of a large truck. Guards from the security company surround him. He speaks into a bullhorn.

Not many names will be read. Usually only twenty or thirty.

He thinks about the day ahead. There is a birth. Rounds at the hospital tent. Deliveries of medicine from the security company. Other supplies he'll need to get from the gang's dispensary.

Their life back home had, for many years, been so very normal. He'd had a small practice but also worked at the hospital most days. His wife worked as a curator at the history museum. Her specialty was the art of primitive people and early societies.

On weekends, they had dinner with friends.

Neither of them had family. Or, at least, family that they any longer saw. Hers dead. His already moved north.

The only sadness was their inability to have children of their own.

He thinks about the teenagers he treated. The dying boy. The pregnant girl. Had he and his wife had children when they wanted to, the children would now be that age.

He wonders if they too would have ended up like this.

No one would mean for this to happen. Yet this camp and the city they left and the towns across the countryside, all are filled with children on a course toward utter despair. Launched on that path unintentionally. But that is the path they're on.

Names are called.

In the crowd, when people hear their name, some cheer loudly, some go silent, some just sink in place, to the ground, hands spread over their damp faces.

Most people whose names are called aren't here at the announcement. They'll be found in their tents. The announcements are a formality, a public expression of false and unrealistic hope.

In the years before they left their home for the border, the violence rose and rose. Rising exponentially as rival gangs and competing law enforcement—the local police, the federal police, the army and special forces—all fought one another in a cycle that was often more about retribution than any achievable, measurable gain.

Kidnappings. Bombings. Drive-by shootings.

The violence was no longer confined to the people working in the drug trade and to those trying desperately to fight it. It had become, instead, a commonplace infection throughout the entire country.

The demand, from the north, grew unabated, unrelenting. A pull that no one in the north has committed to diminishing.

And so, the homes of police chiefs were all firebombed, their surrounding neighborhoods going up in flames.

Midlevel drug traffickers were assassinated in big restaurants, the passersby, the patrons of a café, all caught in the heavy gunfire.

The desperate focus of the police on ending the drug trade soon left regular criminals, the thieves and murderers and rapists, to move about unwatched and undeterred.

Finally, he and his wife had to leave.

Names are called.

A man comes up to him, holding his arm. The man has recognized the doctor. He thinks his arm is broken. The doctor checks it. After a minute, he tells the man the arm actually isn't broken. He carefully pulls the man's shirt sleeve off of the bad arm. He ties it into a makeshift sling.

"The elbow is sprained," he tells the man in Spanish. "You'll need to come see me tomorrow at my tent. Okay?"

The man thanks him. Wanders away. Milling about like all the thousands here, each of them waiting for their names to be called.

The doctor wonders why he comes to these announcements. He looks down at the dust at his feet. Kicks at it. Small clouds rise.

Names are called.

But not his own. Not his wife's.

He watches the dust in the air near the ground. It circles above his shoes.

He remembers how she smiled, eyes wet. Kissing him. As she was above him.

The dust settles. He can see each speck, one after another, finally reaching the ground.

He closes his eyes again. Then moves on throughout the camp.

• • •

Photos from an airplane as it passes close to a mountain. Passengers, the flight attendants, everyone leans toward the left side of the plane. Phones out, although very few people have cameras with lenses. All take pictures of the snowcapped mountain.

One man, where he sits, he can't quite get a picture of the scene outside the window. Instead he ends up with a photo of the stranger in the seat next to him, a woman; in the photo she holds her phone, looking at a picture she has taken of the mountain outside the plane.

He pays for sex.

He gambles his money away.

He struggles with pills. Going months without them. Then telling himself he deserves something more.

CHAPTER 12

THE RESTAURANT MANAGER

Cities on fire.

Built out into the plains, now drier and hotter than ever before. Yards brown. Trees dead.

A simple ember from a backyard barbecue can set blocks of homes ablaze.

• • •

He holds a plastic cup, drinking iced tea. No sweetener. He's gotten to the restaurant early. A different one this week. That's his job. Rotating through each location. Checking on what the workers need.

He glances down at the cup. Clear plastic. The restaurant name and logo printed on the front, wet with a haze of condensation he absently disrupts with his thumb. Along the bottom edge of the cup, words are printed. Many. He finds that he is squinting. The words aren't so much printed as stamped into the plastic mold.

The type of plastic, the manufacturer's name, a serial number, the cup's capacity.

Embossed plastic letters that no one ever wants to read.

This restaurant was built in an area of downtown that the city has tried to redevelop. Bringing stores here. Restaurants. Attractions for kids. Bars for adults.

Most haven't worked. This restaurant, he knows, most months it only barely turns a profit.

The wind blows even harder here as it funnels through the narrow spaces between tall buildings, focused with a force that often keeps people from walking forward. Instead they turn a corner.

Take the long way. It's much easier.

The wind is why this area failed. It has driven so many people away.

He sips from his tea. No customers right now. But they'll have a small lunch crowd in another hour.

On the light posts outside the window of the restaurant, banners fly. Tattered now. Barely attached by wires that rattle and whip and ring out as the wind blows hard across them. He watches a banner, trying to piece together the words once printed on it.

TOMORROW'S CITY . . . TODAY.

•••

Suburbs left blackened. Smoking and decimated. As if bombed out. A leveled city, a cratered village, or is it the surface of a moon?

•••

At night, the documentary about the city that was abandoned is on the television again. Its repeat schedule must meet up with his habits after work. He's seen bits of it a few times lately. He grew up near the city, in its twin city to the south. Newer, the twin was not abandoned.

But the northern end of the city finally declared bankruptcy on its debt. Its pensions had long since gone insolvent. Its employees had been fired. City services finally ended. Buildings were allowed to burn. Video from a helicopter shows a home in a once nice neighborhood, the flames of a fire ripping through the house's roof. A father of four hauling bodies on his own out to the curb. Standing there. Neighbors watching. And still no one ever came to help.

The restaurant manager grew up fearing that place. And fearing the few people who stayed, like that father on the TV screen and his now dead wife and children.

136

That's what happens. It's sad. But that is what happens there.
He moves slightly in his chair. Repositioning.
Why would someone ever choose to stay in a place like that?

. . .

Fires in blighted buildings. An insurance play. Or a homeless camp out of control. Or kids, bored teenagers, with nothing else they want to do.

. . .

He and the girlfriend break up. A mutual decision. There was nothing wrong. But, for neither of them was there much interest in the other.

. . .

Forest fires covering hundreds of miles, moving with a will of their own through rural towns and midsize cities, fire so hot and so fast they create weather systems of their own. Massive planes, tankers filled with chemicals and water from a lake, make bombing runs on the fire lines, again and again; the planes entering the tall, sheer walls of smoke, disappearing as they approach the fires, like small birds gone over the horizon.

His mother calls him most days. Sometimes twice a day.

She wants to go home. Back to her country. She no longer wants to be here? He tells her about the violence there. About the stories his cousins tell.

We can't go back, he says.

She cries into the phone. Sentences that mix Spanish and English.

I want you to help me, she says. *I want you to help me go back home.*

CHAPTER 13

THE CAROUSEL OPERATOR

Trash as an industry. Shipped by rail and by barge. To other cities. Other states. Across oceans. Into oceans.

One hundred and thirty million cell phones thrown into garbage cans every year.

• • •

He does not know himself anymore. What he once was, he isn't. What he's moving toward has no definition.

He sits on the edge of his carousel. The epileptic sits next to him, holding a tower of blue cotton candy at his mouth. The tip of the cotton candy whips around in the wind, back and forth, till finally the wind simply bends it to the side.

"Have you seen the trees here?" the epileptic asks, his lips and tongue turning bluer as he chews. "How they're bent over? Like a kid's book. Some crazy world without colors where everything is bent to the side."

The carousel operator nods. They're sitting behind a sleigh on the carousel, sheltered from the worst of the wind. But still it blows hard on them. Enough that they have to raise their voices to be heard.

No one has come to the carnival tonight.

"It happens," the epileptic says. "It's a school night. Maybe no one heard we'd come to town. There's not a lot of traffic here. So not many people have seen us." He shrugs. "It can happen."

139

The carousel operator nods. He's learned tonight that, on balance, he'd rather work his ride than sit here doing nothing.

"Why'd you leave your friends?" the epileptic asks him. Once again, he presses the big wad of blue cotton candy toward his face.

The carousel operator shakes his head.

"They find religion?" the epileptic asks, chewing. "Express some desire to repent for their sins?"

He's smiling some as he chews.

The carousel operator shakes his head again. "Man," he says. "Man."

The epileptic laughs. "Okay," he says, finishing his chewing. "Okay. They were your friends. I know. I know."

The wind washes away most of the noise of the carnival. The sound of the games. The music blaring from the unused rides. All the normal sounds are carried away just as they are created, so that it sounds as if the carnival were happening not here, but half a block away.

The carousel operator says, in a moment, "There were things that happened," then pauses. His hair whips around his face. He pushes it back. He says, "Things I won't describe."

The epileptic chews. In a moment, he says, "Tell me something."

The carousel operator looks away, toward the coin toss games. A carny throws quarters at bottles. The wind drives the quarters upward, to the side. The carny's laughing. Throwing quarters into the impossible wind.

The carousel operator looks back at his friend. Right into the epileptic's eyes. The first time he's done so. The epileptic hadn't known this.

But now he does.

The epileptic stares back. He doesn't chew. Doesn't speak. He feels the air blow, the cotton candy shaking in the wind.

His friend still stares.

"You didn't know them," the kid says finally. Staring still. The kid can feel it. What it does for him to stare into this epileptic's eyes. "You didn't know them," he says again, leaning toward his friend. "But there's a way in which we had come to believe that none of us could ever die."

The soot and smoke of diesel oil rising from the massive ships that sail the oceans.

Flotillas of plastic bottles, drawn together, miles across, and there's no plan, no intent, no will to clean this up.

Drift nets fifty feet deep and fifty miles long, left to float with the current, ghosts now, that haunt the ocean, collecting millions of animals not intentionally, not to eat, but by accident, entangled animals, all of them left to die.

• • •

He hits the man hard, in the throat, then moves to the side as the man doubles over, the man holding the side of his head, shocked somehow, that he could be hit in the throat.

It's been a week since the last fight.

The epileptic watches this. But does not understand. He's on the ground. Shaking. A seizure having overtaken his whole being.

They're in a bar again. In a small downtown. Hitched a ride. The epileptic once more wanting to try to see the real town.

Not a big crowd here. Maybe twenty people. Thirty. Some playing pool. Most sitting at tables.

One of the TVs is showing helicopter footage of the flooding. The buildings falling over. They play that over and again. But also the damage left behind. Footage of the low wall of water pushing its way across flat, muddy farmland. Water pushing cars off a highway stretching northward, water pulling people from their cars, water overtaking those who try to outrun the wave. Still others are standing on a small, muddy hill next to a church. An island, it seems, surrounded by mud and water, the group on the hill just watching the helicopter as it passes by.

But some of them on that island, the little kids especially, start slowly waving their arms.

The fight started when the epileptic put his hand on the carousel operator's arm. Like he was going to use his friend's arm to stand. But he just held it. Tightly now. The carousel operator turned to him, the epileptic staring forward, white spit forming at his mouth.

"Hey man," the kid said, standing, voice rising as he talked toward the bartender, "I need a wooden spoon."

The kid leaned the epileptic down to the ground. The epileptic's body was frozen, except for his shaking hands. The bartender handed the kid not a spoon but a wooden stick, a drumstick, and the kid took it and shoved it into the epileptic's mouth. He had the epileptic on the ground now. The epileptic was groaning low, but his hands weren't shaking hard, only clenching now, fists so tight that his fingernails dug into his palms.

Some guy nearby had started laughing.

The carousel operator was kneeling down over the epileptic. But he looked over at the laughing man. "Stop," he said.

The guy said, "Can't handle his drink."

The carousel operator stood, staring at the guy. "Stop," he said.

The guy flipped him off. "Fuck you." He was wearing a bright yellow T-shirt, a big guy with a thick chest and his forearms covered in tattoos, a snake tattooed around his neck.

The kid looked down at the epileptic. Biting so hard on the drumstick that the kid could see slivers of wood separating off, getting caught on the epileptic's lips.

The guy with the snake tattoo tossed a piece of ice at the epileptic.

The kid stepped quickly, crossing the ten feet to the man in the yellow T-shirt just faster than anyone can later remember, already hitting him even before the man could stand up. He's a huge man, twice the kid's size, and the kid knows somewhere that he can't let the man get up. If he lets this man stand, the kid knows, knows without articulating a strategy or a plan, he knows that this man could hurt him badly.

So he's going to hurt him first. Render him lame.

He's hitting the guy in the throat, again and again even as the guy is still sitting in his wooden chair. The chair has arms, which is good because otherwise the man would be able to slide out from under the kid's swinging fist. But instead he can only duck his head down, raise his arms, try to stand straight up, but the chair's pushed against the table, so that now the guy in the yellow shirt is like an overgrown child strapped into a high chair.

The kid keeps hitting him. In the ear when the man turns his head away, in the face every time he tries to stand.

Again, there's blood everywhere. Again, there's the screaming. The guy screaming not so much in pain yet, but in frustration at not being able to stand or get away.

The guy has friends. But they haven't moved. Frozen, as they stare at this kid standing over their friend, hitting him so many times that it doesn't seem possible this wasn't planned long ago, some fight come to life as a result of long-hurled insults or a lifetime's grudge.

The kid's hand is covered in blood. His own blood. And the blood from this man.

The man is still stuck in the chair, bouncing side to side, trying to get out of it. But the kid has put his foot on one of the horizontal rails on the chair, is pressing down on it, so the chair won't move.

The guy bobs left and right and forward.

But slowly now. Dumbly.

The kid can't feel his hand or arm. He just keeps swinging. Right arm only. Again and again, hitting the guy twice each time. As he swings down at the man's face. As he raises his hand to swing again, the back of his fist knocking the man once more in the throat.

One of the friends stands now. His haze or hallucination broken.

The kid wheels around, pushing the friend with both his hands, hard, in the sternum, so that the guy is rocked back, stumbling, falling over his own chair, onto the concrete floor. The kid kicks him in the ribs, then the neck, then the side of the head.

Behind the kid, the man in the yellow shirt still bobs side to side. Slowly. Hands half raised. Fending off an assault that he doesn't know has ended.

The other friend, the third at the table, he keeps looking around.

The kid kicks the man on the ground again, in the back, again and again, till the guy on the ground simply struggles to breathe.

The kid now looks at the third friend. The friend's hands are on the table. Ready to stand.

The kid takes a breath, another, holding this one for a second, closing his eyes, another second. He shouldn't pause. He knows this. But he does pause. He waits.

And when the kid exhales, a moment later, he exhales hard, a kind of scream, that blows blood and spit from his mouth all across the table.

He yells at the third man, "Don't fucking stand!"

The kid is breathing hard, shoulders rising with each breath. The blood across his face is from where he's bit his lips. No one hit him. No one touched him. He simply split his own lips in three places, biting down on them as he beat those two men unconscious.

The third man stares. Hands on the table. Ready to stand. He's been told, his whole life, that you always stand.

"I'm telling you," the kid says, more quietly now, almost a whisper, a voice that's all air, he can barely breathe, snot from his nose running across his cheeks, his eyes are wet and red, "please, I'm telling you to please don't fucking stand."

• • •

Pig shit, massive pools of it held in ponds carved out of the dirt, shit slowly seeping into lakes and streams and groundwater, shit-borne bacteria spreading from hog farm to spinach farm to reservoirs to city drinking water.

The rainbow-colored sheen of oily pesticides, collecting now in the drainage ditches at the end of furrows plowed into the fields.

Cattle sometimes butchered while they still stand, staggering but alive, workers too callous or disinterested or just too numb to care that the maul no longer kills the animal they stand before. Instead, the blood of that creature, bits of live flesh and functioning organs, it all runs into drains on the concrete floor, washed down, bypassing filters long since disconnected, entering the sewers, is it alive still when it finds its way to the nearby river?

. . .

They walk into the wind. Between dark buildings that seem to concentrate the force of the air.

The epileptic stares ahead. "Most people only say they were bad," he says. "But they don't mean it. Or if they mean it, it's not real."

The carousel operator leans forward as he walks. Wind pushing harder against them. "It's real," he says.

The epileptic nods.

They walk under banners attached to streetlights. The area is mostly empty. Stores closed. Only a burger place seems occupied. A crew cleaning the floor and counters.

The banners flap loudly, their metal wires hitting hard against the poles. TOMORROW'S CITY . . . TODAY.

"You can die, you know," the epileptic says. "All of us. We can die."

The kid nods. He can still taste blood. From the cuts he bit into his lips.

He thinks for a moment about the girl. Back home. He barely knew her. Quiet girl. Certain of something, though he didn't know what. They had sex. Different sex than he'd ever had before.

He's not sure if he loved her. He's not sure how he would know.

"We go north tomorrow," the epileptic says. "Toward some city that's been abandoned."

They walk in silence.

"Sounds like a real moneymaker," the epileptic says. "Crowds and crowds, I expect."

The carousel operator turns to him. Shakes his head. "Man," he says. "Man."

"You and me," the epileptic says, "we've put ourselves in the hands of a real visionary operation. My future, it seems bright."

The carousel operator shakes his head. Spits blood. The epileptic sees him barely smile.

"And yours," the epileptic says, "yours is just unlimited."

The wind blows heavily, in their faces, against their chests. They lean forward, step after step; it'll take twice as long to return to the carnival as it did to leave.

"All of us," the epileptic says. "All of us can be killed. You know that, right? We can be killed. And we can kill others."

The carousel operator turns to him. The epileptic stares.

"And each time," the epileptic says to the kid, "you almost do."

• • •

Cities where, every day, people must cover their faces with masks because of the pollution.

Cities where children and the elderly aren't allowed to go outside for weeks and weeks.

Cities where coal plants burn unfiltered, the smokestacks casting shadows across houses and parks and schools.

To breathe is to taste. Plastic, smoke, rotted wood. It lingers in your throat. It pours freely through your nose, finally coating your tongue. The flavor of eventual disease.

He walks past churches. Sunday mornings. Wednesday nights.

He walks past them to hear the music. The words of the priest. Repeated. He can mouth along with them.

Long held memories.

He likes the sound of everyone standing. Lifting themselves, a slight step; there's a wind almost, the force of combined motion as they all now stand in place.

CHAPTER 14
THE DOCTOR

Massive flocks of geese land in the ponds in city parks, the birds battling for space to drink and bathe in the water. The geese come by the thousands, hour after hour, some soon rising to join the flocks still passing overhead, other geese staying on the ground for hours. In just a day they'll drain the ponds of water, leaving behind only the mud and their droppings and the lame, dying geese who can't travel any farther north.

. . .

He hears about the flooding all along the Gulf. They get newspapers here, and he's able to afford a phone, and there are makeshift restaurants, set up in tents, with televisions tuned to sports or to the news.

He sits now, in the evening, in one of the restaurants in the camps. His wife did not want to join him tonight. This happens. More and more.

It's not about you, she says. She just doesn't want to go out.

He eats chicken and rice and drinks a reasonably good glass of wine. He watches the Spanish-language news. Reports from the Gulf. Flooding in all directions from the earthquake and the hurricane. To the south it was the storm, not the earthquake, that did the worst of the damage. Wind and rain pushing onto the mainland at top velocity, killing tens of thousands in just minutes. Wiping out the coastal towns. Flattening the lush resorts overgrown and unattended for so many years, their remnants finally washed away.

Mudslides in the coastal mountains killing thousands more, people buried alive where they slept or prayed.

Hundreds of thousands of people have been displaced. Their homes destroyed or rendered too dangerous to inhabit. They wander the streets. Countryside. Pleading with reporters and cameramen for help.

The doctor watches. Then reads more about this on his phone. Then drinks from his glass of wine.

He knows that such a storm, that type of damage in the south, it will send even more people fleeing north across the border. To the wall near here, where they'll try to buy their way through one of the many tunnels. Or they'll pay to board one of the hundreds of boats traversing the Gulf illegally.

The news reports shift to the damage in the delta. Cars fleeing a wave making its way up a highway. People stranded on the overpasses, or hills in farmland, buildings in the city. Buildings that soon collapse.

He drinks again. It all leaves him breathless. The buildings falling over. The mudslides near where his parents lived before they died. The prospect of people, men and women and children, all moving north in greater numbers. So many will die. In the heat of the desert. At the hands of smugglers who will abandon them at any moment. Or on the small boats that flood out into the Gulf, frantically trying to bypass the ships that patrol those waters. Boats overloaded, captained badly by men who have no training or ability, just a desire to make money off the desperation of so many fleeing people.

An hour later, back at his tent, his wife is not there. She's left a note.

Gone for a walk.

He undresses. Gets into his small bed. Turns the lights out. And now he pictures the people, all heading north. He remembers the faces of those who fled with him and his wife when they made their journey. Poor, wealthy, uneducated, children. So many babies. He asked an old woman to lean on his arm for at least two days. Finally, she could not keep up. She was alone. Traveling by herself. She begged him to let her stop. He left her to sit in the narrow shade of a dead tree along a road.

With his eyes open or closed, all he can picture is the people.

He wishes his wife were here. He wonders where she's gone. He wonders if she's safe. He wonders when they will be able to leave.

• • •

Algae blooms spread through lakes, ponds, the fenced-off reservoirs of the largest cities. Green and slick along the surface of the water, or brown and thick and barely visible from above, the blooms spread for miles, a hundred feet deep. Fed by fertilizer, phosphates, an excess of nutrients. The algae dies nearly as fast as it can spread, creating masses made up of tons of dying matter, clogging creeks, clogging shorelines, clogging pipes meant to bring water to nearby farms and towns and cities.

• • •

In just a week, the camp begins to feel the arrival of people displaced by the storm.

The doctor treats them in the hospital tent. Some of the wealthier ones come to him at his tent, having learned already where they should go for extra care.

They have injuries of all kinds. Broken bones from the impact of the storm. Feet so blistered from the march across the desert that toes and heels and soles are infected, bloody rotted messes pulled painfully from their boots and socks. Bodies sunburned and dehydrated from days out in the Gulf. Eyes damaged when a person fell into waves thick with all that oil from the collapsing rigs. Another man's hair is still stained and tangled with crude oil; the man picks at it as the doctor checks his eyes. Heart patients, cancer patients, diabetics, epileptics, all of whom have gone days or weeks without their necessary medication.

But for many, what they need is not medicine or bandages, not splints or ice or crutches. What they need is care for their minds. What they've been through they can't yet describe. Accept. Or believe.

They stare blankly at the doctor. "I don't know what's wrong," they'll say. "I just need your help."

150

The doctor works sixteen and twenty hours a day. At the hospital or in his own tent. And still the lines grow longer.

Periodically, a gang member will find the doctor. Motion to him. It is time to go to the other tents. A group of girls has arrived. They need checking. This, they make clear, will be his immediate priority.

Fifteen of them. Dark-haired, olive skin. The girls are beautiful. They are sought out, across many countries. Other girls are brought through other camps. Girls and women who are shipped off to the mining settlements and oil fields north and west of here. To live out of cheap motels. Motor homes or trailers. There to service the seasonal, transient workers who man the equipment that pulls fuel and minerals from the ground.

These girls, though, in their white dresses, are all sent to the cities. High end. Many thousands of dollars a night. Some are sold outright, to wealthy men who put them up in their own apartments. Some are even married off, becoming one of many wives of a single husband. Soon they will have children. Living as mothers to babies they had no choice in birthing.

"Where will I go?" one girl whispers as he listens to her breathing.

English. Perfect English.

The doctor shakes his head. "I don't know."

"Can you help me?" She is whispering.

He is quiet for a long moment. They rarely ask for help. By the time that they are here, in this camp, they've been broken. Their hope of escape has been wrenched from their hearts. He's not sure how. Or what the gang members do to break them.

Sometimes he will see bruises. Even cuts. But that's rare.

Instead, the girls, if they do talk, tell stories of being kept alone in pitch-black rooms. In the dampness of isolated basements. In the backs of panel vans droning constantly across pitted roads. For weeks or months, they were kept in these places. They aren't sure how long.

But it's been made clear to them that there's only one way to escape the torture of a timeless darkness. Only one way out of the hell that's been created for each one of them.

Compliance.

151

"Can you?" she whispers, in her perfect English, so that none of the guards will hear. "Can you help?"

He's checking her pulse. The closest gang member is thirty feet away. Outside the tent.

"If you try to leave," he whispers, "they will hurt you."

"Yes," she whispers, "but I can try."

The doctor checks her reflexes. Looks inside her mouth. Shines a light into each of her brown eyes.

"Please," she is whispering.

He pauses again. Staring at her. In a moment, he says, "I cannot."

"I am fifteen," she whispers. "I don't want this to be happening."

He nods. "I am sorry," he says.

"You could do something," she is whispering. "Who knows if it would work. But you could do something to give me a chance. Even the smallest chance."

The doctor thinks about all the words that he could offer. How they could be said. He blinks his eyes shut. How do you tell a person to give up? He opens his eyes.

She still stares at him. "But," she is saying, no longer whispering, simply talking to him before he can speak, "it's obvious that you won't."

• • •

Insects so small they're barely visible, spreading through hemlocks and fir trees, slowly stripping them of their needles.

From inside the forests, it's now possible to see the sky and moon and stars.

From outside the forests, the once dense and green foliage is thin now, brown, and dying.

• • •

The camp is overflowing. With people from the Gulf. The security firm has begun to do more patrols through the camp. The gang has become more visible throughout the tents.

The new people must be brought in line.

A man is caught stealing from one of the makeshift restaurants. Like all private enterprise in the camp, the restaurant pays fees to the gang for security. The man, caught with food in his shirt, is beaten bloody in the street, then dragged by gang members, mouth bound, hands bound; they drag him by a rope tied to his feet. A mile they drag him, across rocks, dirt road, over timbers laid down to mark off one neighborhood from another. There's a sign on him, handwritten in Spanish.

Thief.

Within a few days, construction starts on an addition to the camp. Construction workers in crisp, corporate uniforms begin to outline the wooden foundations of more tents. Laid out in long, neat rows, the addition will house thousands of people. Progress is quick. The workers efficient.

Most of them who do the work, they are brown-skinned. From the south.

Only sometimes do they glance toward the existing camp.

Few if any have legal documents.

The doctor stands at the wire fence. Watching the construction for another few minutes. Then he makes his way back to his tent.

His wife is gone again. The note says she's gone for a walk. It's the same note, in fact. One she's written before.

He knows he should not worry. But he does.

When later that night she returns, he tries to tell her about the addition to the camp. "They've begun an expansion," he says. "Which should help."

She turns to him. Still standing. Staring. "We've come to a place," she says quickly, "where it is easier to build tents than to let us live freely. That is not a form of help."

He looks away. The air tonight is warm, almost hot, but the breeze blows.

"Where do you go when you walk?" he asks.

She doesn't answer for a minute. "Nowhere," she says. "I just walk."

That she's lying is clear to both of them. But it's also clear he is not to ask anything more.

"I love you," he says.

She nods.

"We'll get out of here," he says. "I promise. We will."

She nods.

"It will just take a bit more time," he says.

She leans toward him, touches his head. Looks closely at him. Then gets into her bed.

• • •

Parks overgrown with fast-growing privet, flowers choked off from water and light, young trees subsumed, native undergrowth left to die in the shade of a plant once used as a barrier or hedge.

Lakes and rivers swarmed with mussels from thousands of miles away, brought here on the hulls of ships, now killing off the other shellfish in this lake, sucked into water treatment facilities, clogging water pipes as the mussels grow and multiply inside them.

Roadsides covered in vines across mile after mile after mile, coating telephone poles forty feet in the air, enveloping stop signs, fences, shrubs, and trees, creating scenes that are now dying still lifes, deeply green silhouettes of what it is that once stood here.

• • •

He watches the boy die. Lying on the table. Infection. His feet were cut terribly in his walk across the desert. His grandmother stands next to him, holding him until finally his breathing stops.

He watches the girl die. Lying on the table. Bronchial pneumonia. Two weeks in a crowded container, a long steel box shipped into this country; most people died en route. Others, like this one, survived a few days more.

He watches the woman die. Childbirth. The doctor's hands and arms are covered in her blood. The newborn dies as well. Malnutrition. The journey north. The will and strength to complete such a trip. But still not enough to survive.

At home, he sits in a chair. Sipping from a glass of wine.

It's cool tonight. By comparison.

His wife is gone. She's gone every night now.

He knows he should be worried. But he thinks still about four deaths. In one day.

Even now, all these years later, one death will upset him.

Four has left him numb.

He stares toward his wife's bed. The sheets. Just one pillow.

In his mind, he absently runs through the faces he can remember. The people who have died in his care. Not just in this camp. But back to his time at the hospital in the city. The clinic in the countryside.

He does not want to think of each face. He simply lacks the ability to stop.

He pours another glass of wine.

When his wife comes home, she holds a large, tan envelope. She sets it next to her husband.

She sits. On her bed. Looks up at the ceiling of the tent.

"Many people died today," he says.

She doesn't look at him.

"Children. An infant. A mother."

She still stares upward. A beautiful woman. Long dark hair. Olive skin.

There's blood all across her hands. Dry. Her fingers and palms stained dark. They are almost purple.

He thinks he should stand, walk to her, check her hands. A doctor. Something is wrong.

But he doesn't. Instead he looks at the envelope. It isn't thick. But it bears the official seal.

"What has happened?" the doctor asks.

She lowers her head. Stares at him. Dark eyes. She doesn't smile. She is beautiful.

Her hands, dark with blood, rest on her bare knees.

His wife. The drug lord's daughter.

Dark with blood.

The drug lord's daughter.

"They were never going to let you out of here," she says now, in her perfect English—it's been years since he's heard it, and now it's as if a stranger speaks to him. "You are much too valuable to them."

He holds his glass of wine, suspended where he was lifting it when he first saw the blood.

"But I could no longer live here," she says.

He loves her. But he hardly knows her. Met when they were twenty-five. She'd lived overseas.

"You have many abilities in this camp," she says. "So much that you can offer. And you've done so. Which makes me proud. I'm sorry I haven't said so. But I am. Because I love you."

She still stares at him.

"However," she says, "while I do have great value to the world, here in this camp I have only a few abilities to offer. And as I did not want to give my body over to anyone but you ever again, there was only one other thing that I could do. One thing to buy our freedom."

The glass is heavy in his hand. He should set it down. But he can't think where he would put it.

"The violence was about to come here," she says. "With all the money and trade that flows through these camps, the gangs would not leave each other alone forever. They want in on each other's territory. Always. That will never end."

He's still silent. He stares at her dark eyes. Her long, dark hair.

"The violence was about to come," she says again.

She blinks. The first time in many minutes.

He'd always thought they ended up in this specific camp by chance. But he's realizing that isn't so.

"There were only four," she says. "That was the price."

He shakes his head. "Who?"

"Men," she says. "With history. Come here under false identities. Wealthy. The wealth of the drug trade. And so many people shipped to the north. All with ties to other gangs."

He looks down at her hands again. Stained with blood. They rest on her knees.

"I was able to get close to them," she says now, staring. "But don't worry. You have no reason to worry. They only looked," she says. "They didn't touch."

The wine has dripped all across his white shirt. Red stains, circles of red, like blood soaking out from his chest and stomach. Like the blood from the woman who died with her baby, blood that covered him; it felt like it covered all his body.

"We leave tomorrow," she says. "We must go far to the north. That's the one condition. We must go far away."

Perfect English.

"I never knew," he says. "Never thought," he gets out.

She stares. "It will be okay," she says. "If you love me. Then it will be okay."

He nods.

"I cannot stay trapped here," she says. "I cannot live trapped again. For too much of my life, I was trapped."

He nods.

She stands. She undresses herself. Steps forward and takes the wineglass from his hand. Her fingers, darkly stained, move the glass so delicately. With such grace. Setting it on the table.

"Lie down," she says, removing his shirt.

"Hold me," she says, before she kisses his mouth.

"I need you to love me," she says, as she presses her face against his neck, both naked now, quiet movement, he loves her, more than he'll ever be able to say. He loves her, holds her. He has never really known her. He's always realized that. But she loves him.

He loves her.

He's just never really known her.

"Always," she says. "Love me."

• • •

157

Fish pulled from the ocean with such speed and efficiency that, this year, virtually none will survive the winter.

Whales hunted methodically, across the polar cap, until no more can be found.

Primates squeezed into such small areas that they themselves have finally decided that they will no longer breed.

He dresses the body of a prostitute. One he'd frequented from time to time.

She was killed. *By some customer,* they said.

But he is sure it was her pimp.

His finger traces the track marks along her toes.

Her mother selected the girl's pink dress.

He tries very hard to make her pretty.

159

CHAPTER 15
THE RESTAURANT MANAGER

Goods of all possible types, stacked neatly under the bright lights of this warehouse turned into a store. There is food, and there is lumber, and there is soil in bags and fruit in bags, and there is clothing and footwear and ice. Quartermaster to the masses, a limitless supply of all that anyone should ever need.

• • •

In a bar, after work, he sees a man almost beaten to death.

It leaves him shaking. In his seat near the bar. Police and an ambulance come. They ask for descriptions of the men who did this.

"It was just one guy," the bartender tells the police. "Some skinny kid. White. Never seen him here before."

The restaurant manager sees his hands shaking. When he can, he gets another drink.

He stares up at one of the TVs still playing behind the bar. Baseball. Bright colors. The motion of statistical graphics, replays, a bunt, an out.

He turns away. Too much motion. Too much color.

The kid hit the man so many times. So fast. The man not able to stand. Get away. He just rocked back and forth with the motion, finally slumping over against the arm of the chair.

When one of the man's friends stood up, trying to help, the kid beat him so badly that he was laid out, on the ground, within half a minute. Less.

The other people in the bar simply stared. No one stood to stop it. No one stood to help.

All anyone could do is stare.

Throughout it, the restaurant manager sat on his bar stool. Looking over his shoulder. Watching at an angle. Not realizing that he could turn his body fully around, he instead only turned his head, his hands still resting in front of him, on the bar.

Now, as he pictures it again, his stomach churns. All that blood. So much blood. The two men not just beaten unconscious but injured terribly.

"What happened?" a guy behind him asks.

The restaurant manager doesn't turn.

"Fight," the woman next to him says. "More like a beating."

"Why?" the guy asks.

"Some big guy started throwing ice at someone. Some guy who was having a seizure. On the ground. Foaming at the mouth. Big guy sitting over there, where all that blood is, guess he thought it was funny. Threw some ice at the guy having the seizure. Black guy. On the floor."

The man behind the restaurant manager says, "Damn. God damn."

"Fucked with the wrong person's friend," the woman says.

"Damn," the man says again. "God damn."

The restaurant manager tries to tune them out. Looks up at another TV. Updates on the flooding along the Gulf. The city there decimated. The farmland washed over with water and debris. He's seen the footage twenty times. Its effect now is not to horrify or to scare. Now it only numbs.

He looks down at his phone. Text messages. His fingers shake. He can't quite get the messages to open.

The kid was so violent. So much blood. Covered in that man's blood. It wasn't like a movie or a TV show, a couple punches and the man goes down.

This man would not go down.

And the kid, he wouldn't stop.

When he was a child, the restaurant manager had a neighbor, another child, maybe six or seven years old. He liked to torture cats. Stray cats, his own cats. He'd tie things to their tails. Shoot at them with his pellet gun.

Once the restaurant manager watched from his window as the neighbor beat a cat to death with a simple, heavy branch.

This was the same.

So brutal. So empty. Devoid of a decency the restaurant manager has never articulated, but that he had otherwise always assumed all the people of the world want to share.

• • •

TVs lined up side by side, ever larger, flat black screens. Some are widely curved.

Refrigerators, one after another, blurring finally into the ovens, the dryers, the washers, the microwaves, and the air conditioning units, and the silent dishwashers costing hundreds and thousands. Silver and white and black, more cycles, more features than it seems possible to offer. Or that could ever be used.

Computers, by the hundreds, the size of briefcases or folded up so small they'll slide into a purse. More power, more capacity than the computers that launched rockets and capsules and humans all the way to the moon.

• • •

Outside, in the morning, the wind blows even harder than usual. He can barely open the door of his house.

The news blames it on the remnants of the hurricane. Even a week later, its dissipating power spreads out across the country.

There are tricks to living with this wind. He parks his car parallel to it, with the driver's door facing east, so that he can open and close the door without the wind smashing the door back on him, or wrenching the door against its hinges.

Driving, he feels the wind, it bounces the car around even on neighborhood streets. But he always knows now, without thinking about it, where the wind is relative to his position. Even turning onto busy streets, he has to account for the gust blowing against his side; it wants to push him into the wrong lane. He pulls harder on the steering wheel, leaning the car into the wind. Like sailing a ship along Eighth Avenue.

The restaurant crew is all on time. This is not a small thing. Crews like this, for these restaurants, the simple act of getting the employees here is part of his job as manager. Helping his employees navigate the mediocre bus system. Helping them arrange to get their children to first or second grade. Helping them find free clinics for sick family. Siblings, parents, or their children, the people who work here tend to be the ones in charge of everything.

Those who are from south of here, he doesn't look too closely at the quality or accuracy of their IDs or documentation.

They work hard. They are here on time. They simply want to help their families and themselves.

He works with the crew as they get through the breakfast rush, talking the new people through their jobs, helping at the cash register when they need it, hauling trash out, working the grill, going out to the drive-thru line and greeting customers with small samples of the store's new coffee drink. He hands the cups through open windows, very carefully; the wind wants to knock these drinks to the ground.

Only later does he have a minute to check his phone. Text messages from his brother.

His mother is sick. Hospital. He needs to go there. He needs to go there right away.

• • •

Rows of small, plush beds of many different sizes.

Aisles adorned with grooming supplies, the brushes and scissors and soaps and sprays, all hanging carefully from long hooks.

Food stacked in bags and boxes and cans, ever more expensive as the aisle moves right to left, food raised and processed and bagged with a care beyond comfortable description.

A few hours of driving north, and still the car is bouncing, shifting, pushed against by the wind.

The restaurant manager's mother is very old. She's lived longer than he or his brother ever thought was possible.

A good woman. Who did her best for them. He's not close to her. She hasn't ever allowed that to be possible. But she's a good woman. Who deserves to see her sons right now.

He finds he is replaying the fight in the bar. The beating, really. It wasn't a fight.

But his stomach doesn't turn. His hands don't shake. He simply replays it. Again. Not meaning to. It's just what his mind has decided to do.

He'll travel north a few hours more. To the city where he grew up. The vast suburb to the much older city from the documentary. As a kid, he was only told the stories. *We live in the South End. Across the highway is the North End. Do not go there. Do not play there. Do not let your friends dare you to enter that place.*

This was even before the area had been abandoned. A hundred thousand people still lived there then. Schools were still open. He once drove with his mother through the North End to the old church cemetery where her mother and father were buried. What they drove through was a worn-out, emptied place, storefronts dark and boarded up for street after street after street.

But once the last of the schools finally closed, once the last factory shut down and the police left and even the city mayor walked away from his job, then the city died.

Yet many of the streetlights still operated. The traffic lights blinking green, now yellow, soon red.

The documentary said some few thousand people still live there. In homes they've owned their entire lives. Or in homes they've simply taken over for themselves. Still others have gone there to salvage things of value. Copper tubing, aluminum gutters. They strip down homes and buildings, scavenging items of some value to buyers in the South End.

Why would someone live there?

Hours later, he still drives on the highway. The fight no longer plays in his mind. A memory worn down, details steadily blurred, edges smoothed away by constant repetition.

In a moment, he can see it, as he comes up over a slowly building rise in the otherwise flattened landscape. Ahead there are the clouds. A line of gray that lifts upward at a sloping, intermittent angle, three miles it goes, disappearing into the sky, having started so low to the ground that it's as if the clouds spring forth from some unidentifiable source within the earth. In thirty minutes more, he'll reach those clouds. Passing into a place that, starting some fifteen years ago, has been enveloped, that lives under an almost constant rain, that has not seen any sunlight since the manager was in his teens.

He'd been a boy, really. Just thirteen. Waking up one day to a storm that poured water all across their yard.

The rain did finally break. Days later. Just a mist continued to fall.

But the clouds, they still hung there, in the sky. And never left again.

• • •

Shoes priced in the thousands. Jackets priced for thousands more. Purses, watches, outerwear, all priced like collectible items of the future, treasures of cultural significance, not utilitarian objects of need.

He wakes up. Nearly dead. Drugs again. Getting worse.

He has a moment where he stares. At the air conditioning unit barely lodged inside the motel wall.

He will have to leave. Everything and everyone.

He will have to leave. If he's going to continue to live.

I will have to leave. Right now. This moment. Get up. Go. And leave.

He can think of only one place.

He dresses. Gathers a very few things. Soon, he crosses the overpass. Entering the city that's been abandoned.

PART 3

PERMANENT DUSK

The boy talks about his day. Telling his mother about a game they played at school. A game on the playground after they'd done art, and he hopes that tomorrow they'll be able to sing.

He loves when they can sing.

First grade.

His mother nods. Smiling down at him as they walk. About a mile they walk. From the bus stop to their small home.

And still the boy is talking.

CHAPTER 16
ARRIVAL

Scientists seek funding for further study of the cloud mass. Politicians use its existence to their relative advantage. Those few news reports that still cover what happened discuss this only as a phenomenon unexplained. It started many years ago. There's not much more to say.

The people who live under the clouds, they have simply found a way to adapt. Or they'll soon choose to leave.

• • •

His daughter sits in the backseat making dandelion bracelets from the weeds she picked at a gas station a few hundred miles behind them. He watches her in the rearview mirror. Carefully bending each stem, interlocking them, the yellow flowers evenly spaced along the natural chain that she's created.

She's making four of them.

"I want to keep one for Mom," she says.

Five days since the buildings collapsed. But still he hasn't told them.

I'm sorry, but your mother has died.

He drives. Wind pushes hard against the driver's side of the car. He feels like he's leaning the car into the wind.

They are heading north. To the city where his parents live.

Back on the highway in the delta, it took ten or twelve hours to navigate the labyrinth of abandoned and destroyed cars. The horror of slowly driving through that maze of abuse numbed all three of them.

Cars and trucks wrecked.

Dried mud and debris covering all that they could see.

Bodies twisted inside and across the vehicles.

He and his kids drove along in silence. Sometimes just a few miles an hour. The smell of rot and chemicals dissipating only after half a day of driving.

Although some part of him wondered if the smell actually faded or he and his children simply grew accustomed to the scent.

Sometimes they'd drive ten minutes, twenty, then realize there was no way through the cars ahead of them. Having to back up to find a different path, in doing so once more witnessing the same row of bodies bent sickly, dirty, in the shoulder of the road.

Finally, they reached the end of the damage. Suddenly, with no hint it was coming, they reached the end of the car wrecks. The northernmost edge of the flood. A hundred and fifty miles from the Gulf.

They kept driving. Unable to stop in a few small cities already overloaded with refugees from the storm. They slept one more night in the car, then finally reached a city not overwhelmed with refugees. The three of them went to a massive store in a strip mall to buy fresh clothes. Then checked into a hotel room across the street. They took turns showering. They washed clothes in the laundry room of the hotel.

"We don't usually let the guests in here," the manager said to him. Pausing. Looking him up and down. Seeing his armload of filthy, dirty clothes. Seeing the man's children standing behind him. Knowing. Knowing where they had been. "But, sure," the manager said. "Of course."

Other people, like them, did the same. Buying clothes at the huge store across the street. Using the laundry. Eating full meals in the chain restaurants all around them.

The father and his children passed these other people in the hotel lobby. In the bright, chain restaurants nearby. But no one spoke of what they'd seen. No one did anything more than nod.

An experience still unspeakable.

Finally, late that first night in the hotel, his kids got into bed. Sharing a big queen bed, they curled up tightly, their father reading a book to them for almost an hour. Then they fell asleep, slowly sprawling out, sleeping through the morning, to the afternoon, still sleeping as the sun finally set once more, and he felt for the first time since his daughter was born the need to check on them. Are they sleeping, or have they somehow suddenly died?

He held a finger under his daughter's nose. Then his son's. Breath across his fingertips. He touched each of them on their backs. Feeling their hearts beating quietly. Slowly. In the silence of this hotel room.

Crying now.

Safe.

Now he could finally cry.

This went on for some time. Just the sound of his breathing in the otherwise silent room. Rough. Broken. Crying as quietly as he could.

Then he got into his own bed. And slept for hours and hours and hours.

• • •

The North End of these twin cities underneath the clouds died many years ago. Inattention. Fiscal abuse. Mismanagement. Fear of change. Broken industries. Polluted land and water and air.

In many ways, the North End of the city was dying long before the clouds enveloped it.

But the South End of the city grew. Flooded with people who fled the decay in the north. Attracted by the promise of safety, low taxes, the aura of normalcy and the new.

They sit side by side, twin cities created by a wide highway dug deeply into the ground. A trench, with walls reaching sixty feet down.

Now, there's only one overpass left to cross it.

A dislocation and separation made normal by time. And forgetting.

• • •

The doctor and his wife sit silently. They ride a bus heading north on the highway. Sitting in seats near the back. One small backpack each in the rack overhead. His wife has a purse. He has a wallet and his papers in his pocket.

That's all they own. In all the world. Forty years since they were born. This is the sum total of their lives.

She holds his hand. Or he holds hers. It's not clear how it started. But for a hundred miles now, they've held hands.

He wonders, worries, thinks constantly, about what he could do better.

She does too.

The bus's restroom smells of urine and excrement and the sour byproducts of decomposition.

He wishes it didn't smell bad. He wishes none of this were so. They worked so hard. Studied for years. Found jobs that made a difference in the lives of people they knew and never met.

His nose again recoils at the scent of the toilet near them. Sometimes, when the air in the bus drifts this way, his wife will cough. Cover her mouth.

There's a city they've been sent to. A city where they are now allowed to live. This was a part of the bargain she made. The price of killing those four men.

He knows she did not like it.

He knows she wants something so much more for both of them.

But, now, he knows what stands in the way. Her history. His. They have to escape their history.

He's breathless. Broken. Hopeful. Numb.

It changes with every mile.

She holds his hand. He holds hers.

There's hope in that.

More hope than he can define.

She leans toward him. Says near his ear, the first time she's spoken in a hundred miles, "What will we do? How will we live? Do you understand what we have done?"

He nods. Instantly. Immediately. *Yes.*

"Of course," he says aloud.

Exiled. In trade for freedom. Exiled, to a city where the gangs have no presence. And no interest.

She holds his hand. More tightly than before.

The things she's done, he doesn't picture them. The four killings. Her life before they met, now revealed. He does not picture this.

As long as she will hold his hand.

He can see the wall of clouds ahead of them. A storm front stationary, simply awaiting their approach.

Rain begins to spray against the windows next to their seats. The bus is shaking now, lightly, then loudly, its massive length bending some; they can see the passengers in the front of the bus shifting left as he and his wife shift right, the bus seemingly squeezing itself through an opening much too small.

It gets dark outside. As if evening suddenly fell.

She says, looking out the window, "I think we're almost there."

• • •

The area to the south is known as the South End, a tan, suburban landscape of new and low buildings, massive houses built on winding streets, subdivisions without sidewalks, vast and plain apartment complexes spread across land that's been bulldozed flat and cleared of trees.

And across the fissure of the highway cut through this place in the North End, is a city once home to more than a million people. A city where now just a few thousand people live, wandering an emptied urban landscape. Miles and miles of a right-angled grid of streets and homes and offices. Gothic hospitals, ornate museums, grand churches, and a cathedral. The few residents walking from place to place within the North End find escape, or they find routine, or is it just that they find silence?

• • •

He assembles his carousel in the rain.

As always, they've set up in a shopping center parking lot near a highway.

It's midday. The carnival won't open for hours. He wanders away from the rides. The rain is not really drops. It's a mist. A dampness that, if you don't focus on it, you wonder if it is falling or rising from the ground.

Feels like home. His home. Far to the west of here.

Imagine weeks of this. People don't understand. Driving cars a hundred miles an hour along roads slick with a mist that's been falling, blowing, seeping from the trees, for days and weeks and months.

Forty days without sunlight. Sometimes, it'd go fifty.

There was a hopelessness in that rain. A sense that no matter what you did, you would not escape.

He's standing next to the highway trench, leaning forward on a steel guardrail as he looks down at the eight lanes spread out sixty feet below him. Cars move, small trucks, massive semis en route from places a thousand miles from here, pulling huge boxes, silver tankers, some pull equipment wrapped in canvas and plastic, protected, and the words on trucks and the cargo they pull is indecipherable as the carousel operator leans over the highway wall. Staring down.

Vehicles move east and west.

People, in all of those cars and trucks. This strikes him. A thought. That he's never had. All these people. Each with their own lives.

He's never much considered this.

He fled home. He left everything he could behind. But the world he found, the one he lives in, he feels when he feels anything that this life has been created just for him.

It's not beautiful. It's in no way perfect. Very little of it does he like. Instead, it's a life he slowly steps through, scenes fashioned palely from the ether of his solitary experience.

But, still, he managed to escape.

His face and hands, his wrists and neck, they're coated in the cool, damp mist. His hair too. Water drips past his wide-open eyes.

He stares down into the highway. At the faces. Faces of the drivers he can only barely see.

He feels no anger.

He feels no pain.

He wants nothing to go badly.

He just stares down into the highway. Glimpsing faces. A crew of men heading to a job. Passengers on a bus. Women on cell phones driving semis pulling fuel. Women and their kids in a minivan or SUV. Fathers and their children in cars indistinguishable from one another.

He'd like to never fight again.

He'd like to never inflict damage of any sort.

He'd like for the willingness to harm to dissipate. Disappear.

That he's never killed a man, the epileptic's right, it's more luck than anything.

And as always, he thinks of the girl. Pictures her in the small cabin of an old fishing boat. On sheets printed with cowboys riding ponies, cowgirls riding horses. Sex that wasn't like anything he'd done in the back of a car or out in the woods.

He wonders where she is now.

He wonders what she does.

It's been two years. Since he saw her.

He wonders how he could talk to her.

He wonders if she'd answer his call.

He says her name to himself. Then he closes his eyes. The noise from the highway rises wildly past his ears. It's everything, louder now, with his eyes closed; it nearly dizzies him. He holds tight to the highway rail. He won't be knocked aside.

But the noise of this highway is as loud as anything that he's ever heard.

• • •

A man still picks up garbage. In an old, municipal dump truck he repaired and maintains himself, he drives through the old neighborhoods in the North End.

He doesn't call out. Doesn't honk his horn. Yet, somehow, everyone knows that it is trash day.

176

. . .

In the airport, she follows her analysts as they walk through a tunnel that bypasses normal security. Access to and egress from the private jets that land.

Not that there are any other private jets here. But this is an essential part of the game. Build private entrances for the wealthy in order to exceed their expectations.

The boy, though, is somewhere above her in this airport. She flew him here on a regular jet. An element of secrecy. But he had a seat in first class. He had never flown before. Now he's a flying god.

The boy has his own room. In the hotel where they all will stay.

He texts her that he's landed. She texts back. *Good.*

She's never before given one of them her actual number.

She and her analysts flew in and she could see the abandoned city from the airplane window. Miles of it. Gray streets, gray buildings, leafless trees leaning to the side. She wonders which of it had come first, the gray across every surface of this place, or the rain and clouds that cover it?

She walks. A big SUV awaits them at the end of the dim tunnel. Black, of course. Tinted windows.

She'd prefer to avoid the silly pretense.

Why highlight that she has more money than millions of people in just the surrounding area? She has more money than all but a few people in her company. She has more money than all but a few thousand—maybe it's ten thousand, maybe it's a hundred thousand—people in the world.

Isn't this just happenstance? Some inexplicable mix of genetics, luck, and timing?

She looks down at her phone. Wonders when the boy will text her back.

A thought she's not ever had.

She follows the three analysts to the SUV. A man in a black suit opens the door. A small headphone, on a curled wire, hangs from his left ear. Beneath his jacket, she sees his gun.

This makes her smile some. Who, anywhere, would want to do anything to her?

She climbs into the vehicle.

177

Bags are piled into the back.

The SUV has been modified, made to be a sort of limousine. She and her three analysts sit facing one another.

She doesn't prefer this to be so. But she'll manage.

The boy has still not texted her. It makes her feel frustration. Of a kind she has not felt before.

"What do we see first?" she asks her analysts.

One of the analysts, a woman, dark hair and very smart, probably the smartest of the three, says, "We have a helicopter tour scheduled for tomorrow morning."

The woman presses back against the leather seat. Seat belt in place. That the four of them have buckled up inside this massive vehicle seems to her somehow comical. Even though she doesn't know how to make a joke of it, she's sure that everything about this SUV is silly.

"That's fine," she says in a moment. "But, at some point, I'd also like to drive through the city. Not just fly above it."

The female analyst nods. "Of course."

They are silent. The SUV has started driving. They are facing one another. Something that, in four years, they've never quite done before.

The woman's mind runs through comments she could say out loud. But she doesn't say them. None of them seem quite right.

She closes her eyes.

She'd rather be cooking dinner for herself tonight. In her own apartment.

But she'll be eating dinner at the hotel with her analysts. Another chance to face one another.

Only later will she go to the hotel room. A very nice room. Like the rooms she picks in her own city.

But she has clothes there for him. Bras. And panties. And a dress. They wait for him. And for her.

She looks forward to the evening.

But now she opens her eyes. Looks at the two analysts across from her.

They stare.

The analyst beside her stares at her too.

It strikes her suddenly what she should say. "If there's no money to be made here," she says, "that's fine. We'll have visited this place. Seen something that we've never seen." She pauses. She glances out her window: they're descending an on-ramp, accelerating as they enter a walled and sunken highway, rain spraying across the outside of the windows. "And then we'll go back to the office. And find another way to multiply our money."

• • •

Empty schools, with equations still handwritten across chalkboards at the front of the class. Homework assignments listed with their due dates. The portraits of past presidents line the plaster walls.

One day, students were taught to read. The next day, no one came to open the school's front doors.

• • •

They sit in the small, dark bar in the lobby of the hotel. She drinks. He does not. This bothers her very much. Acting more mature. Like he's more in control. Implying somehow that she's the problem.

The private detective is running late.

On the walls are photos of the city across the highway. Before it was abandoned by its residents. Black and white, printed five or six feet across, it's a city of streetcars and big theaters and brightly lit streetlights shining down on broad avenues filled with people.

She takes another drink.

Her husband orders water.

She wants to scream at him.

How can this private detective be so late?

He arrives twenty minutes later. Apologizing, he gets a drink, they sit down in low chairs around an even lower table. He begins to tell the story. The story of their youngest son.

Prostitution, drug addiction, moving from city to city. He has pictures on his computer. Photos of their son entering a drug dealer's house, random cars under an overpass. Photos of him placed in offering on websites for women and men.

Her husband begins to cry. She just watches the faces move across the screen. Distant shots. Of a person vaguely familiar to her and her husband both.

None of this is real.

She orders another drink.

The detective keeps on talking. Monotone. He must do this often. He seems practiced. Experienced. Numb.

"Your son stays not far from here," he says.

Her husband looks from the detective to his wife. "We can't just walk up to his front door," he says. "Barge in, then what?"

The detective shakes his head. "He doesn't have a front door. He only has a back door."

The wife lets her head turn slightly to the side. Staring at the detective. Finding her gin. *Why could that possibly matter? To anyone at the table.*

The detective continues. "What I recommend," he says flatly, "is that you arrange for treatment. A place that will accept him. Give consideration to your insurance, his specific needs. Then there is a service you can hire. Transport. It's a type of service."

They know full well of transport. Their oldest son, twice, they had to hire a transport service to get him from their home to a distant treatment center. Three people. Very big. Very strong. Seizing him. Wrestling their son to the ground. While the parents and the youngest son watched from the hallway of their home.

She looks at her husband. Sees the face of her dead son.

"What's the address?" the wife asks.

The detective has it written down. He pulls a paper from a folder. Sets it on the table.

"Will he be there now?" the wife asks.

She's done transport. Watched it twice. In her home.

Not again.

The detective nods. "It's still early," he says to the mother and father. Sipping from his drink. "He hasn't yet gotten his drugs. And he hasn't yet gone to work."

· · ·

Two men and a woman drive in a pickup truck across the North End. Toward a neighborhood. They now park. Get out. Go into the house. Join others who strip copper tubing from inside the gypsum-covered walls, copper wires from inside ceilings, copper pipes from the water heater and the furnace and the appliances.

Other people do the same. Fifty of them. Stripping raw materials from these homes. Dropping all of it in massive piles. Near the street. Leaving all of it for the buyers who will come soon. Seeking the scavenged remnants of a neighborhood left behind.

The near silence of how they work is hypnotic or haunting, or maybe it's only calm.

· · ·

He sits in the waiting room of the hospital. His older brother sits nearby. They don't talk. They've talked earlier. Now, they're just waiting for their mother to die.

They both stare down at their phones. He does so only as a motion with which to occupy himself. He's trying not to cry. Not in front of the nurses. Not in front of his older brother.

"Hey," his brother says, nodding toward their mother's room.

Two nurses are leaving her room. The brothers stand, then return to their mother.

She raises her hands as they enter. Smiles wide. But weakly. Too weak to speak. They stand, on each side of her. Each of them holds one of her hands.

She does not want the TV on. The room is small, quiet except for the hiss of oxygen fed to a tube running underneath her nose.

She closes her eyes. To sleep. Smiling. Holding her boys' strong hands.

You are all I've ever loved.

• • •

Air-raid sirens sound off throughout the North End, on a schedule no one can decipher. A civil defense system meant to survive a nuclear attack, its decades-old computer still triggers the sirens. The wailing screams from church steeples and the roof of an old hotel and from tall and vacant office buildings in the long-failed business district.

Even a few minutes later, the rising then falling sirens still echo emptily across the city.

CHAPTER 2

CROSSING

She starts each day at 4:00 a.m., getting her son's things ready for school.

She puts food into his lunch box. Sets it next to his small backpack that he leaves, every night, next to the front door to their small house.

She goes into his room while he still sleeps. Makes sure his clothes are out. And they are. Every night, before he goes to bed, her boy always does that too.

She watches for a moment as he sleeps. Blanket tucked between his hands. Tiger pressed against his cheek.

She watches. A moment more.

He has to walk to school alone. But, she thinks, the bus stop is only half a mile away.

Then she leaves, in a moment letting herself out the front door of their small home.

CHAPTER 17
CROSSING

It takes a moment. Sometimes a few minutes.

For others, it takes an hour. Even more.

But eventually you will realize that the city isn't just abandoned.

Actually, everything in the city, all the trees and grass and flowers once planted around buildings and homes and stores, all of it has somehow died.

• • •

His kids ride the carousel with him. He has always preferred a ride like this. The rides that flip upside down or whirl about at high speed all make him motion sick. The rides with height scare him badly.

Tonight, his kids agree. They have no interest in the small roller coaster or the catapult cages shooting passengers up into the air. Even when he pointed to the teacup ride his daughter said quietly, "Not tonight."

Mostly, the three of them have only walked around this small carnival near his parents' house. Alternately overwhelmed and relieved by the noise. They walk. Not talking. Only looking at the games and cotton candy machine and the other people jumping into and out of the rides.

He and the kids arrived here yesterday. For a stay of what duration he doesn't yet know.

Insurance claims. Government filings. Bank accounts. Health insurance. Will they stay here or go someplace else? He'll need a job. They'll need a house. The kids will need to be in school.

He needs to tell the kids that their mother died.

The young man who runs the carousel stands on a platform in the center of the circling ride. He's a kid really, staring up. The father glances at him, then watches for a moment. The kid is still staring straight up. For a full minute. The father sees him intermittently, as the ride keeps circling round. The kid's face is bruised near his eye, and the father notices one hand is red and cut and wrapped in a small and awkward frame. A home-made splint.

There's a realization in a carnival or at a fair that you've put yourselves, your children, everything, into the hands of someone who hates what they do. Who is barely paying attention. Who is not in any real sense trained for the job they have.

His daughter rises and falls on the unicorn. His son does the same on a tiger.

He thinks of the friends of his who must have died back home. Coworkers. His neighbors. He lived there ten years.

How many people did I meet in those ten years? How many of them are dead?

The ride circles. The father stands, hand on a pole. Steadying himself.

His apartment building may even still be standing. All the things he owns could be fine. The toys and clothes of his children. Furniture he'll want some day, need when he figures out where they can live. Memories embedded in a painting on a wall. A lamp even. Certain clothes.

Or maybe it was washed away.

Who knows? How to find out? What exactly should I be doing?

His son, on the tiger, reaches out to his father. Holds his hand. No reason. His son's not afraid. Doesn't want down. He's not sad. He's not smiling.

He just wants to hold his father's hand.

• • •

A few hundred people scavenge abandoned homes and buildings. Day after day. They sell what they strip and tear and wrench from these structures to men and women in white panel vans who park along the street.

Faces pale with gypsum dust, arms bloodied from scraping them against broken timbers and rusted vents, necks scarred from cuts inflicted over months and years of work.

Often they go hours without anyone speaking aloud.

• • •

She wants the boy between her legs. In his bra and panties. She rolls over. Pulls him onto her. Wants him close. Touching her. Kissing her. She wants him now and she'll want him later, pushing into her, in his slow way, such a beautiful boy.

"Please come. Please now."

She showers in the morning. In her own room. Where she brought him. Now she dresses. It's quiet. Top floor. Suite. They said this was the quietest room in the hotel. That is all she asked for. Quiet. Which brought her to this sprawling room overlooking the new end of the city.

From the other side of the suite, though, there's a window where she can see the vast neighborhoods of the abandoned city. They call it the North End. She stares out at a broad, sculpted avenue that leads from neighborhoods to downtown. Buildings rise there, in a cluster.

How can a city die?

The boy sleeps in her bed. She watches him. How he breathes.

Downstairs, she eats breakfast alone in the hotel restaurant.

Across from her, a man cries. Quietly. Into his hands.

He sits alone. Table like hers, at a window; they've inadvertently ended up facing each other across their separate tables.

He can't stop crying.

She drinks her cappuccino. Eats two poached eggs. A piece of bacon. One piece of toast. She drinks another cappuccino.

And still he silently cries.

She reads a paper book. About the history of oil. The rise of petro states worldwide.

Periodically, she looks up.

He still can't stop himself. He holds his face in his reddened hands.

186

After a time, a woman sits down with him. Wife. Blocking the man from view.

The wife doesn't talk at first. At least not to her husband. She orders breakfast. Coffee.

Soon, though, she's talking. A voice that's only air.

Only venom.

The woman looks up from her book about oil. The deals made to establish whole countries.

The man leans his head back. Staring up at the ceiling. His wife breathes venom. Words the woman cannot hear.

The woman stares at the back of the wife's still head.

She knows that sound. She doesn't even need to make out the words.

It's her father's voice. Her father's sound. Her father, before school, after, that is the voice her father had. Breathing fire at her day after day.

The man crying reminds the woman of her mother. She's realized this. Not that she ever saw her mother cry. But her mother sat, silently, absorbing the fire spewed at her every day. Never once doing anything to stop it.

She wishes, the woman does, finishing the last of her cappuccino, signing her bill, checking the page she's on in the book about oil, she wishes her mother had once stood. Told her husband to stop. Done something. Something to stop or halt or even barely diminish the assaults her father continually launched.

But she didn't.

The woman stands. Gathers her things.

While the wife breathes fire.

The man still cries. Even though there are no tears now. He doesn't hold his face. Actually, he's only looking at his wife. Still. Face blank.

But clearly, inside, he cries and cries and cries.

• • •

The water tastes like water once imagined. Cold and bright and with a feeling, not a taste, but a feeling that you could drink this water your entire life.

It runs from the taps this way. Everywhere in the North End. The water tastes like something you haven't otherwise ever found.

• • •

The doctor looks at his wife. They've walked into the hospital. A city hospital. In the South End.

Maybe they have a job for him.

Not as a doctor. He has no license in this country. It will take a year or more to get approved for that. But he knows his way around a hospital.

The clerk looks over his application. Human Resources. "Don't you want a job as a doctor?" she asks him.

He sits across from her in a small cubicle. His wife waits outside in the hall.

"That's not yet possible," he says.

The clerk nods. "That's a shame," she says. "We need doctors. Always we need doctors."

The doctor nods too. Smiles slightly. "So what do you have?"

She looks at her computer screen. Scrolling. In a moment, she says, "Orderly?" She repeats the word, turning toward him. "Orderly."

He nods. "That will be fine."

She looks at his application again. Then at him. "Okay. We have to do background checks. Run your work papers. It will take a week or two."

He nods. "Everything will check out fine."

She looks at him. "I wish I had time to hear your story."

He smiles some. "Another day."

Outside, in the hallway, he and his wife stand together. Where to go next? There is a college here. Maybe she can work there, she has said. But from what they can tell, this South End is not a place with things like museums. Art galleries. Even the one college here doesn't have an art or art history department.

They've been exiled to a place unable to embrace their skills.

As they turn off the hallway toward the elevator, two men stand in an alcove. Near the elevator doors. One is weeping. The men embrace.

The doctor looks around. He sees a sign for the hospital's morgue. One of the men, the older one, holds a clipboard. Paperwork.

Transfer papers for the just deceased.

He and his wife get on the elevator with the two men.

The men are clearly brothers. The facial shadows of shared parents.

The younger one wipes his eyes on his sleeve.

The elevator doors don't yet close. The four of them stand and wait.

"I am very sorry," the doctor says to the men.

Both men glance toward him. Nod. *Thanks.*

His wife, though, steps toward them. Hugs the older man. Holding him a long moment.

The elevator doors close. The floor begins to lift. Slowly. The elevator is old, its motions so methodical.

His wife moves to the next man. The younger of the brothers. Hugs him also. He begins to cry again. Into her shoulder. He can't stop. He just cries. His whole body shakes. Crying. Long past the time when they've arrived on the first floor.

• • •

The abandoned factories hold vast supplies of raw materials, chemicals; there are spare parts. Warehouses stacked fifty feet high with never used tires. Thousands of them. Covered in dust. Left here a decade ago. Factories whose holding tanks are lined with layers of gold, filaments of platinum strung inside clear glass tubes.

Wealth and value decommissioned, left behind as people and businesses fled this place.

• • •

The woman walks ahead of her husband. Down a faceless street of tiny duplexes. Triplexes. Short apartment buildings just two or three stories high.

189

To her left, the highway roars. A sound whose source they cannot see. A constantly rising sound, it drowns out her steps, her breathing; increasingly it drowns out her thoughts.

She likes it, in her way. No thinking. No worry. No madness.

She just walks.

The streetlights above the highway turn everything they see to a faded gray or white.

Her husband taps her shoulder. She turns quickly. Wants to slap at his hand or face or body. Anything.

He steps back. Is saying something. She can't hear the words. The sound of the vehicles is far too loud.

He points. At a house on this narrow road paralleling the highway.

It was once a tan house. Gray now. Very small. Built cheaply between two, low concrete apartment buildings. Probably the house was built before the apartments. Only now does it look out of place.

The small shrubs planted on both sides of the concrete porch are dead. Sticks. Sprouting up and out. A thin plastic bag clings to a branch. It shakes and billows outward, whipping wildly.

The woman realizes there's a wind. Rain. She's soaking wet. Her hair sticks to her forehead. Chin.

Her husband points to the house again. To a path along the left side of it.

She goes to the path. A walkway made of small concrete pads, laid intermittently in the mud. They find the back door. She turns the knob. It's unlocked. She walks into a living room made from a dining room. The house has been cut in half, arbitrarily; the wall that cuts through it divides a window on the wall. On the floor is carpet, low, aquamarine with swirls of texture. The couch is brown. There's a TV. An old one. Big. It sits heavily on the floor.

Her son sleeps on the couch.

And the woman starts to cry.

She has not cried in years. Not since before her first son died. Not since some trip to another institution in another state. A flight, a rental car, a well-manicured lawn surrounding a low building outside of town. Another

190

meeting with the therapists, case workers, a selection of young men and women who'd exited this program. *It changed my life. It will change your son's.*

It didn't.

But it did make her decide that she would never cry again.

Tell yourself you'd do better.

Tell yourself you'd find a way.

Tell yourself the mom's the problem.

Tell yourself she makes it worse.

Tell yourself the dad's the problem.

Tell yourself he makes it worse.

Tell yourself your love for your children and your faith in your spouse would never falter, never change, never exit this landscape that's been created without warning or invitation. A world unknown. Without empathy. Without care. Stripped of connection. No forgiveness. A world that knows no mercy.

Live there. Year after year.

Then tell yourself you could still cry.

Or tell yourself that if you cried, you could make that crying stop.

Her son wakes up. Looks at each of them. They stand across from him. In his half of the living room.

He's impossibly thin. Arms exposed, as if ejected lamely from the sleeves of his thin and graying T-shirt. Red lines, or are they black, scraped up and down his skin, trajectories only he can follow, cutting paths of pain and blood and failed relief all across his body.

"Go away," he says quietly. Still lying there. Prone.

The father looks around the room again. The mother cries.

Their son sits up, feet now pressed against the horribly stained and worn-out carpet. "Really," he says flatly. "You should go away."

• • •

Although buildings and factories are slowly stripped down to their bare walls, few homes are scavenged in the North End. Only those that stand in the

191

last neighborhood built there. A modern subdivision, nondescript, unlike any other neighborhood in the North End. This subdivision was built after the highway was constructed, the subdivision covering the remnants of a vast park split in half by the straight, deep trench that cut the city in two.

The scavengers not only strip these homes of the metals they can sell, they also tear the houses down. Flattening them. Then moving on to the house next door. As if clearing the land. Maybe turning it once again into the park that was destroyed.

Or returning this land to what it had been many hundreds of years ago.

• • •

"Are you looking for something really cheap," the teenaged girl next to them now says. "I mean, like, free?"

The doctor and his wife sit in a diner near the hospital. They have been talking about what to do next. A practical, ordered conversation that is incongruous with the love they feel for each other.

"We have money for a few weeks," his wife has said. "But only if we are very careful."

"There are many jobs, even basic jobs, that we can do," he has said. "We only need to find shelter. Some time. Then we'll be fine."

Now, they both turn to the teenager in the small booth next to theirs.

"Sorry," the teenager says. "I didn't mean to eavesdrop."

They both shake their heads. His wife smiles lightly. So does he.

The girl says, "It's just that you both seem very nice."

She has tattoos across her hands and arms and neck. Her nose is pierced with a silver ring. Her lower lip holds a row of thick, black studs. "So if what you want is something cheap," she says. "Really cheap. Then you just cross the overpass. To the North End. And, well, it's strange. Hard to explain. But you just pick a place to live."

The doctor isn't following what she's saying. His wife squints. Confused.

"People say it's scary there," the girl says. She's drinking coffee. She holds a piece of toast that she's about to eat. "They say it's dangerous. And I used to

192

think that. But then I went over there." She stops to butter her toast, slowly unwrapping the fifth or sixth of the foil-wrapped tabs of butter from the bowl on her table, carefully coating her wheat bread in fat.

The butter is free, the doctor realizes. As is the cream she loads into her third or fourth coffee refill. The jam is free too, and she spreads it thickly across her toast.

Maximum calories, a very few dollars at a time.

"I went over there thinking it'd be scary," the girl says, pausing to chew. The husband notices that she has near perfect manners. "I thought it'd be some sort of crazy thing to do. But it's not crazy. It's not even scary. What it is," she says, pausing, looking for a word, "what it is," she says again and, for a moment, she closes her eyes, "is quiet."

They thank her. Finish breakfast.

Afterward, they cross the overpass to the North End.

Entering a city that's been abandoned.

They walk. Small backpacks looped over their shoulders.

She holds his hand.

He smiles. *It will be fine.*

They walk. Along a broad avenue leading past brick homes two stories high. A boulevard, really, lined now with the slick black trunks of trees that somehow died.

It's a mile to downtown. Home after home. Brick. Wooden. Gothic. Ornate. Simple. Austere. Beautiful.

All so beautiful.

Architects designed these, each one, individually. House after house. Churches made of stone. Lodges adorned with slate. Brick storefronts lined with tiny parapets. More long blocks of homes.

All empty.

"I know nothing of this place," the doctor says.

"I'm not sure where we are," his wife says, now in Spanish. She's spoken English since they got out of the camp. But English wouldn't convey her meaning.

Her husband nods.

193

It rains. But lightly. As if the rain didn't fall but was instead spontaneously created, tiny beads of moisture manifesting themselves before their open eyes.

Downtown, a man carefully sweeps the large set of granite steps leading up to the cathedral. The man sees the two of them. Raises a hand. *Hello.*

Then he goes back to sweeping.

A white van moves slowly down the main avenue they just traversed. The van stops. The driver, an old but clearly strong, deeply healthy man, gets out. He holds newspapers in a bundle. He goes to a metal box on the street corner. Opens the door. Drops the new papers inside.

The doctor watches this in wonder.

There's a bridge across a canal, its stanchions and trusses so ornate and elaborate that you'd think it was meant to cross a grand body of water. But instead it simply crosses a narrow canal.

There are many of these bridges. They can see four or five of them from where they stand.

He sees an empty hospital. A boarded-up city hall. A court building lined with columns; its front doors have been removed. Inside, it's only black. Next to it is a dark museum, then a library, made of stone, soaring four stories tall; on top of it there is a dome.

Next to the doctor and his wife is a small brick building whose roof is gone except for a set of heavy, horizontal beams on which clear sheets of glass have been carefully placed, a ceiling translucent, beaded with the slight and steady rain. Below this, there are tables of a kind. A giant wooden spool turned on its side. A crate. Another crate. Chairs of many types and heights. It's a restaurant, and near the back there is sheet metal, maybe it's the hood of a car, that's been used to form a bar.

Lightbulbs hang from single wires. Bright white lights in the otherwise constant gray. The bare heat of the bulbs creates a steam from the drops of rain in the air.

A few people sit. One raises her hand. Waves.

"We were banished to this city," she says to her husband. "But they did not say which side."

The doctor and his wife enter the restaurant. Set down their bags. Sit at a table.

In a minute, a man brings each of them a glass of wine.

A helicopter passes overhead. The doctor and his wife look up. Through the beams and glass the helicopter is only a blurry image. Yet it's a disruption. Not just of the silence in this place but the stillness. And the simplicity.

That there's even electricity here seems remarkable.

The doctor's phone has no signal.

They sip wine. It's cheap and served in old glass jars, but it is quite good.

"What has happened?" he asks his wife.

But she doesn't answer. She just looks across their crate, smiles lightly, only a little. But, nonetheless, it is a smile. For him. She says, again in Spanish, "I don't know. And I don't care."

• • •

Storms come here. Quickly, with an intensity whose cause scientists still have not identified. Born of the cloud mass that covers this place, or born of the same source that brought the cloud mass here.

Lightning, rain that's total, the air turned liquid as tornadoes begin to spin, wreaking damage all across this empty landscape.

The storms hit the South End too, of course. Tearing not through abandoned neighborhoods, but through new and populated subdivisions whose inhabitants have increasingly decided to search for other cities where they can live.

• • •

The helicopter sweeps out across the industrial area of the North End. The analysts tell the woman about the history of the factories below them.

"This was one of the most successful areas of mass production in the world," the female analyst says. "Many decades ago."

The woman nods. "And the South End?" she asks.

195

Another analyst nods. He's wearing jeans. The woman only now notes this. The three analysts are all wearing jeans.

She wears a suit.

The analyst who is black still nods. "Some industrial production moved to the South End," he says. "But not all of what was here. Much of it simply died. Which means that, in a way the people of the South End don't fully understand, they were dependent upon the North End being a center of industry. Even if the residents moved to the new neighborhoods, they needed the industrial base to remain. But it didn't. Couldn't. Because so many people fled."

The woman leans toward the window of the helicopter. Looks down. Smokestacks. Sprawling factories. Warehouses that go for hundreds of yards, even as their wooden roofs sink slowly inward, in places bursting downward, soaked through from inattention and this constant rain.

"So," the woman says, still looking out the window, "our bet is against the debt of the South End? Municipal debt. But also companies based there that cannot easily move?"

An analyst says, "Yes."

"What about the housing?" the woman asks. They're crossing over an airport. Abandoned. The covered, cantilevered walkways all leading to planes that won't ever again arrive. "In the South End," she says, "there must be a way to bet against the people all living in the shadow of a place like this."

The analysts are quiet for a minute. She can hear them whispering.

In a moment, one of them says, "Housing." She's not sure who has spoken. "We have a way to bet against their homes. A location-specific derivative. Built upon residential-dependent retail, property-tax supported debt instruments, and, of course, every home mortgage we can find."

Outside the helicopter, they pass the buildings in the business district. Office buildings. Beautiful ones. Built of stone and steel, and one is adorned every few floors with granite chimera, each unique, each looking out on the many buildings around them.

They pass another office building. Apartment buildings. Next to them is an old hotel. She can see the rooms. Once beautiful.

196

In one room, its windows are open. She sees a man is standing there. Looking right back at her.

"Why do these people stay?" the woman asks.

No one answers. The helicopter turns north.

Far away, near the edge of the gray horizon, black clouds have formed. Rapidly.

"We'll have to return to your hotel," the pilot says over the intercom. "Now."

The helicopter begins to bank. But she watches the storm as it continues to form. Seemingly fed by the ceiling of gray clouds above them. But also by the water of the sea, or the bay, or maybe it's a lake, located to the north. The water is warmer there. Only slightly. But it's warmer than it has ever been. Warmer than the world seems ready to accept.

• • •

A miracle of engineering, the North End was built on ancient shoreline and wetlands that once flooded throughout the year, a feat manufactured via a series of interconnected levees and canals.

A city created by a system of tidal management that, over the decades, has been almost completely ignored.

Levees fail. Canals overflow.

No one seems to care.

No one seems to know.

And yet the water moves slowly forward.

• • •

The boy runs. Very suddenly. He springs up from the couch, barefoot, in T-shirt and jeans. He is running. Past his mother and father. Out the back door. Gone.

They have to chase him. It's not a choice. Mother and father, seeing this, their youngest son, his disgusting home.

Both of them sprint after him. Down the road that parallels the sunken highway. He runs ahead of them. Half a block. Toward lights ahead of them. Brighter even than the streetlights over the highway, these lights are yellow and red and green, glowing against the sky.

A carnival.

The boy jumps the fence, men scream at him, his mother follows, over the fence, the husband stops, pays the men. Their admission. He talks fast. Pulls more cash from his open wallet.

Lights, strung on wires from pole to ride to the top of another pole standing between three rides. Games, some with bottles, some with water, basketball hoops, large rings, plywood stalls adorned with overstuffed bears and overstuffed tigers and overstuffed alligators of four sizes. Music plays. From every ride. Every game. So that each song intercepts another, walls of sound they pass through as they run, constantly crossing the point where one song gives way to the other.

The mother sees him. Her son. She hasn't lost him. Even over the fence. Through the crowd. She will not lose him now.

The boy runs. All he wants to do is run. He does not know where he will go. He does not know what he wants. He does not know even where he is.

He just wants to run.

As a boy, he hated carnivals. He hated circuses. He hated anything like a fair.

His mother knows this. Thinks this. As she chases her son across the crowded, asphalt parking lot.

Near a ride on the edge of this small carnival, a crowd has gathered. Thicker than what should be.

The boy slams into someone in the crowd, then another person. He thinks he can push through them. Just push everyone aside.

But there are too many people.

In a sense, he's now trapped. Among people all standing still. Pushing together. Moving toward something he can't see.

The boy now wants to scream. So he does. But no one hears. The music is too loud.

The boy now wants to hit something. So he does. But no one even responds. Everyone just assumes his blows are a part of the motion of the crowd.

And he's unable, after all, to hit anything very hard. Weakened. Fading. Wisp.

His movement forward is impossible. He only slides, between people so focused on pushing forward that he can only find small spaces in the gaps between the bodies.

The mother pushes too. Forward. Hard. All her strength. Shoving every person who can be moved.

When the boy, the son, slides out between so many people, he thinks that he is free. But he isn't. He's standing at the center of the crowd. Above two people. Teenage boys. Barely men. One bends over the other. Kneeling. But his arms reach forward, frozen. Suspended somehow. His hands made lame.

On the ground, the other boy, a black kid, he stares blankly toward the sky. His mouth overflows with liquid, white and tinged with blood, and his lower jaw is clamped shut. Jammed against his teeth and lips.

He stares. Blankly. Upward.

Dead.

The boy knows this. Even barefoot. Thin. Standing still on the wet asphalt. The man on the ground is dead.

Across from the son, here in the center of this ad hoc mass of bystanders, the boy looks at his mother.

His mother steps forward, over the dead body. As if it were not there.

It's not that she doesn't care.

She just needs to get ahold of her own dying, broken son.

• • •

No animals either. They've all gone. Not just the dogs and cats. But the birds who lived here or just passed through. Squirrels in the park. Nothing.

All of them have fled this place.

199

The carousel operator looks down at his friend. Kneeling over him. It's so loud here. So many people stand around him.

Everyone he knows seems eventually to die.

Around him, the crowd keeps pushing inward.

But he doesn't care.

He doesn't care even when a woman, he can't understand what she's doing, she just steps over his dead friend. The epileptic. He barely knew the guy's whole name.

The kid stands. He looks up at the sky. Rain falls. His face is wet. More wet even than his shirt and jeans and hands.

He raises them. His hands. Rinsing the epileptic's saliva from his fingers, the blood from his thumbs. He sees bite marks, his blood, or his friend's, from when he tried to pull open the epileptic's mouth, all washing away in the light and steady rain.

The kid looks upward now. There's nothing to see. Just the lights of the carnival. Hung from poles and rides around him. Light reflecting vaguely off the clouds that hang above them.

He thinks that he should scream. He thinks that he should hit someone. He thinks that he would like to drive faster than he's driven before.

But he has no ability to do these things.

None at all.

Why, he wonders, does everyone always die?

He does not hit anyone as he pushes through the crowd. He just moves through them as they part. His tent and backpack are tucked away in a compartment in the center of the revolving carousel. He steps up onto the ride. It carries him around as he walks forward. Months later, and he's still not used to this.

He gets his stuff. He hits the stop button on the carousel.

And now he'll leave. It's time. To go somewhere else. Find some other job. Find some other place.

Maybe he'll call the girl. If he can find her. Maybe it's time to call.

Maybe he could go back. Just to see her.

He's soaking wet. Like he's been all his life. He is soaking wet. Without a plan. But he'll leave here. He'll go somewhere else.

That's what he's meant to do.

• • •

Once awarded for its architecture, the city is now actively forgotten.

A failure no one wants to admit.

To acknowledge it would mean something no one is willing to define.

• • •

As they pass through the hotel lobby on the way to the black SUV, the woman sees the boy. He's a young man. She knows this. Sixteen. Eighteen. Somewhere in that range.

He sits alone in the hotel bar.

Even now he is so beautiful.

She wants to tour the North End in their vehicle. Now, after the helicopter trip was cut short. But she also wants very much for the boy to come to her.

He sees her across the lobby. Stares. Looks down. Now looks up again.

He does not know what to do.

She doesn't blame him.

But she wants him to be with her. A line she'll cross. She's decided. So she waves to him. Waves him over. He'll ride with them.

He's a line she'll cross. Her choice. It's already done.

• • •

Along the highway wall, in the neighborhood cut through a park, scavengers hunt the small, poorly made homes for metals. Sometimes glass of certain types. Unbroken. The people who buy these common treasures, they want the glass in perfect form.

She holds her son. This is something different. Something not allowed. For so many years.

Her husband drives. She sits in the backseat. Her son rests his head. In his mother's lap. What's happening, the mother can't quite understand.

She leans forward without disturbing the boy. Reaches out her hand. Touches her husband's arm.

She's not done so in many years.

• • •

Along an avenue in the North End, a man is walking. He carries an old and heavy camera. It uses film.

Periodically he stops. Before a factory. A school. An old home.

He snaps a picture. Pauses. Then he snaps one more.

• • •

He gets into his car. After hugging his brother one last time. He'll come back. In a week. For the funeral. Their mother wanted to be buried in the North End. He can't quite focus on that yet. But she wanted to be buried in the old cemetery there. Where her family's buried. All of them. Going back more than a hundred years.

• • •

People forget all kinds of things. Ignore them. Relegate it to the other. The different. *It's not mine.*

Poverty. Clear stupidity. A lack of food. Limited water.

Utter prejudice. Violent sexism. Disgust for learning. A rejection of the intellectual.

This city is not alone.

202

In truth, some few say what otherwise goes unsaid.

This city was just the first to fall.

. . .

His kids stare toward the crowd of people. Standing under the lights of the carnival. He touches their shoulders. Touches his daughter, then his son. *Let's go.* "It's time for dinner," he says, watching the crowd across the parking lot.

That's not good, he thinks, looking at the crowd. But it's not an event for him to know.

"It's time," he says. They need to drive. Meet his mother at her favorite restaurant. Miles from here. "Come on," he says, as his kids both lean into him; his boy holds his leg, his daughter holds his hand. Smiling some. Up at him. He says to them, "It's now time."

. . .

The storms over the city, when they come, each time there's a sense that they grow bigger, taller, more severe. It'd be hard to know for certain. There is no comparison. These storms, over a city that's been abandoned, are hard to quantify. Measure. Or even comprehend.

Some nights, when she can, they both sit and watch a movie. She doesn't watch the television. And does not let her boy.

But sometimes she allows a movie.

Quiet movies. Animation.

Some are set in wooded places. Others in ancient cities. Others are in the clouds.

But what matters is the quiet.

They sit in silence. She and her boy. Her boy in her lap. She holds him. As they watch. Scenes unfolding over so much time.

CHAPTER 18

THE HIGHWAY

The first vehicle to wreck on the sunken highway is a large truck pulling two trailers with canvas sides. The trailers are empty, light, and in the wind and rain that's pressing into this man-made trench, the trailers become a set of sails, wobbling separately, yanking against each other, but then the wind builds, the rain as well, and the canvas sides bow inward, purely concave surfaces catching the wind in all its force, both trailers tilting, twin sailboats listing beautifully.

A storm has come. As if launched from a weapon meant to harm.

Storms come often here. Rising off the water to the north. Lightning in them. Small tornadoes.

But this is a storm that casts total shadows. In some places, there's no longer light.

The leading edge of the wind has reached the western end of the highway trench. The trailers tip first, falling over, pulling the truck onto its side as well. The noise would be horrific, except the rain and wind strip every other sound away.

The trailers and the truck are splayed across the four westbound lanes of the highway, looking, from a distance, like a child's toy left in the gutter.

This is where it starts.

The first car to reach the scene is going seventy, maybe seventy-five, when it hits a trailer.

Another car had been following the first car very closely, using it as a guide through the heavy rain, a bad strategy made tragic as it slams into the cab of the truck.

Seventy to zero, in just a millisecond.

The first car held only a single driver, a man, twenty, on his way to work.

The second car held a driver and three passengers. Father at the wheel, daughter and two friends late for practice in the back.

The truck driver had survived his crash, but was killed by the second car.

The third car hits a trailer, careening through the aluminum roof, but stopped immediately by the truck's heavy, steel frame.

Another two people have died.

A pickup truck approaches the scene at full speed, even in this rain, but through the haze of the storm the driver somehow sees the wreck ahead. He veers left, toward the shoulder, the truck beginning to spin then slide in the mess of long untended debris along the highway shoulder. The truck flips soon, twice, then again.

Another driver dead.

More cars come through the rain, undaunted by what seems like just another storm. Some even rushing to escape this part of the highway, where sometimes water builds up, slowing the traffic to a crawl. Four cars seem to fear this possibility, driving faster as the storm descends, a pack of sorts trying to get far from here before things become worse. The first car, driver panicking, manages to weave her way through the wreckage, threading the needle, her driver-side mirror is clipped; it flies off, hits a car behind her. But the other three cars all crash, two sliding sideways as they wildly brake; one hits the end of a trailer, bounces off into the shoulder, then slams into the concrete wall of this highway trench.

Airbags, screaming.

But everyone in that car is fine.

The other car, also sliding, hits another vehicle. The car is now rolling backward, the front seats breaking on impact, hurling both people into the backseat where they crush the passengers.

The next car never sees a thing. The driver hits one of the trailers at full speed.

And the storm has only begun to arrive. The force of it is still north of here. Building. Moving south, as all the storms here do now. Adding to itself. Gathering rain. Gathering wind. Gathering debris from the ground.

In a sense, all that's hit the highway so far is the air and rain that the storm itself pushes out of its way.

The storm moves over neighborhoods and factories abandoned so long ago in the North End. Levees break. Canals are flooded, combining with other canals a block away.

But there are so few people in the North End, that, so far, no one there has died. No one's even injured.

On the highway, there are fifteen dead. Another thirty injured. Almost forty vehicles wrecked so far.

And the wind only rises.

And the rain blinds everyone it touches. West of the city. And east. Even the streetlights lining this highway are of little use, mere pinpoints of light in the violence of the rain and clouds, stars almost, rendered tiny by the storm. The mass of cars and trucks and buses minutes ago had only been traveling through the usual gray dark and constant rain. But now, the storm has reached the full length of the trench. Rain and wind flood over the walls. Darkness. Gusts that snap cars left and right. A violence so far beyond what seemed possible just moments ago.

The crashes are now happening along this entire stretch of sunken highway. The wreckage of the vehicles grows, loosely gathered piles of steel and tires and glass.

And humans. There are injured people everywhere.

Now a semi pulling a tanker filled with chemicals hits the first pileup to the west. The driver had slowed, going forty, or is it thirty; the storm had made him cautious. But he has too much momentum to consider stopping. The cab of the truck hits two cars, killing both drivers who'd until then survived their wrecks. The tanker, sliding outward, to the left, whipping around, breaking free of the cab, moving backward through the vehicles all stopped across eight lanes of this highway.

When the tanker tumbles over, the seals on the tank are broken and a mist releases, upward, straight up, in defiance of the wind.

Yet whatever chemical it is that escapes repels all water, so that the rain that falls, now falls elsewhere, outside the cone of escaping mist that rises from this stretch of highway. The mist is yellow, it sheds water, and for cars not far away, most stopped, some wrecked, others that are only just slowing down, the mist is visible, even with the rain and wind and darkness of the arriving storm.

Cars still wreck, a few more people die, but now, at this end of the highway, everyone has begun to slow.

Brake lights glow from cars and trucks and semis, the vehicles themselves barely visible in the rain, but their lights send a warning to those that follow, sudden and brilliant harbingers of what most people on the highway think is a simple wreck ahead.

A mile to the east, the rain breaks for a few minutes. It has the perverse effect of leading cars there to speed up, even though they are able to see the lighted trail of stopping vehicles ahead of them.

This is just the rain we've had for years.

Another wave of crashing starts. As the cars enter the descending, darkened clouds that continue to reach down into this concrete trench. A few drivers see the lights of the cars stopped ahead of them. But it's too late.

And others are distracted by the sight of a yellow, rising cone some quarter mile away, distinct and unknown in the otherwise gray, enveloping storm.

What is that?

And for them it's too late also.

Twenty cars and trucks have slammed into each other in this new wave. Another twenty will soon follow.

Ten more dead. Three more children.

The screaming is unbearable. But few hear it. The storm, the cars themselves, all of it is just too loud.

And the light, the light of streetlights above the highway and headlights on all these cars and the taillights, all lit red, and the light of buildings and homes in the two cities created by this highway, the storm has progressively absorbed and defeated all this light.

Now, many cars, when they wreck, their inhabitants die in darkness.

The wrecks have begun to occur in an almost controlled slow motion. Cars for miles have decelerated, many have already stopped. Yet throughout the line of vehicles, cars and trucks keep hitting one another. Distracted by the traffic, or the tall and glowing streetlights that now flicker again then go dark, leaving the sunken highway in an even darker abyss, or the drivers are distracted by the cone of yellow mist that rises just ahead of them, or they're distracted by the violence of a tornado that hops from one side of the highway to the other, lifting, suspended above the heads of hundreds and hundreds of people who watch, screaming, but the tornado only jumps, one side to another; the trench in this moment saved everyone underneath that cyclone, because here there are only wrecks, cars careening, trucks that slide across the median; it's total madness here. The impossible come true.

When they take her boy from her, they do so while she's working.

Her whole neighborhood has been condemned. County government. They want everyone here to move. The area deemed a slum. Filled only with the dangerous and the poor.

This is how the South End works.

Anyone left in the houses is sent away.

The elderly are offered vouchers for a shelter. And rides in a run-down bus.

The children are taken under protective care.

It will be weeks before she sees him.

CHAPTER 19

STORM

In the Gulf, the oil rigs still bleed. Two million gallons, oil pouring from the seabed every day.

But also natural gas escapes. Rising from the wreckage of the rigs once used to mine them. One, a well far down in the water, its rig collapsed days after the hurricane. The gas keeps rising, hurling itself through the water's surface, blurring the horizon and the sky.

Now lightning hits the plume, the gas igniting as if it were a bomb.

And so a fire burns brightly from the sea.

• • •

As they descend the on-ramp to the highway, she asks, "If we succeed in this investment, how many people will have lost their homes?"

An analyst taps on her calculator. "At least twenty thousand."

Another says, "And if we top fifty, the returns will exceed the Gulf."

The boy sits in the front seat. With the driver.

The analysts did not ask anything when the boy came over to their table. They introduced themselves. And that is all.

"Then it's worth it," the woman says.

The SUV begins to shake. Then begins to roll. The woman looks up. The roof now seems to bend. Twisting inward. Toward their heads.

She wonders about the boy.

⋯

The doctor and his wife retreat to the church. The huge cathedral. The storm that comes, it's a black wall of motion, holding lightning, tornadoes, worse. He does not know that this cathedral will be safe. But it was the closest building to where they stood.

One half of the sanctuary is lit. The other is in darkness.

Chandeliers shake above their heads. Stained glass windows lose their color, as the little light outside of here is overtaken by the storm.

"We should go to the basement," says his wife.

And so they run.

⋯

The car in front of him lights up red. He thinks he notices much too late. Veering right. Into the shoulder. The road here is covered with debris. Bottles and rocks and tires; ahead of him he sees a helmet. His car slides. Forward. Past cars on his left already stopped, wrecked, a chain reaction pileup.

And just this morning, his mother died.

⋯

He stands at the rail bordering the highway. Looking down into it. Turning his head slowly. Left, then right. Trying to see where he could enter. Hitch a ride. In which direction, he has not yet decided.

The former carousel operator looks up. The noise of the cars and trucks below him is such that there's nothing else he can hear. But he feels it. Then sees it. A black wall just a mile away. Coming toward him. All of them.

He has to remind himself.

You are not alone.

⋯

When the car shakes, then jumps, seemingly lifted from the road, the mother grabs her son. His arm. The closest thing that she can hold.

Beneath her fingers, the boy's arm is rough as sandpaper. With scars and cuts healed poorly. Some bleed lightly now. Triggered by her touch.

The mother cries here in the backseat. But then she's been crying for some time. Crying quietly. As her son sleeps silently against her thigh.

The car slides, sideways. Her husband pulls the wheel left. Now right. The car shoots into the shoulder.

"What?" the mother asks. Very quietly.

Her husband answers. But she can't quite hear him. She can't even see him.

On the highway, day has turned to night.

• • •

There's a lesson somewhere. About bad things. They happen. To good people.

He can't articulate this. He doesn't try. Doesn't want to. Doesn't need to.

But as the cars ahead of him all begin to slide, veering left and right, their red taillights blurring even more than the rain could have caused, he thinks only that he will live today. And he knows his kids will too.

That's what he thinks. Very clearly. A truth he knows.

This is something my son and daughter will survive.

• • •

No effort is made to stop the fires burning in the Gulf. That is a mere problem. Elsewhere, there are dangers. Disease along a coastline without clean water or steady power. Injuries to tens of thousands. Oil that still leaks, pouring constantly from those more than twenty wells damaged in the storm, thick layers of crude already washing over beaches and marshes and islands many hundreds of miles away.

• • •

The SUV rolls again. No one in the back is buckled. The investor hears the airbags trigger in the front seat even as she feels herself slam into another person. She can't tell who. It's only darkness here, and the noise of the car's steel body scraping across concrete drowns out most everyone else's screaming.

• • •

They find a room in the cathedral's basement. Priests' quarters once. Two beds. A small table. A wooden chair. A dim light on the table. A bulb in the ceiling overhead.

They sit. Close together on a bare mattress.

Outside, above them, the storm seems certain to wipe out everything it will touch. The noise of it, thunder and wind and now the storm carries so much debris, large objects, all of it crashing against itself, against the sky, against the city in its path. Even in the basement, the air is wet and heavy. A weight that moves across them. Soon surrounds them. They can feel it, a storm with a presence almost like that of a person reaching down to touch the two of them in this small room.

• • •

The restaurant manager is stuck on the shoulder of the highway. Beside him, through the blur of the rain and darkness, cars slam into one another. Not that they move quickly. But cars behind him, trucks too, they keep slamming into the pileup, pushing all the vehicles together, like bumper cars at the fair.

His car hasn't been hit. There are cars behind him in the shoulder. Cars ahead. But he has not been touched.

• • •

The former carousel operator is being pelted with debris. Even before the wall of black clouds reaches the highway. Bits of things, he does not know

214

what, are flying into his face. Against his hands. He squints, staring into the wind. Across the highway, just a quarter mile away now, the wall of black moves forward. Fast. There's lightning deep inside it. And a tornado springs out from the clouds.

It disappears. Reappears a moment later.

The debris gets bigger. Shingles now, pieces of boards, dead branches, shards of tile and pottery.

He sees shells. He thinks maybe he sees bone.

Finally, he has to turn away. Leaning down. Hiding from the storm behind the wall along the highway. He lays out flat. Covering his head.

And the debris hitting the wall beside him, flying over his head, continues to get bigger. Stronger. Closer.

$$\bullet \; \bullet \; \bullet$$

Their car is hit, from behind. She holds her son.

"Get down," she hears her husband say. She can see him only intermittently. When car lights shine at them. She sees her husband then. And around her she sees the wreckage. Buses crashed. Huge semis turned onto their sides. Cars pointed in all directions.

Then it's dark again.

"Get down," he repeats.

She does. Pushing her son onto the floor. Her son doesn't fight her. The mom lays down, across the backseat. Her son holds her hand. "What's happening?" he asks.

His mom says only, in the total darkness, "I don't know."

Their car is hit again.

$$\bullet \; \bullet \; \bullet$$

The father steers the car to the far left side of the highway. Scraping it along the wall. He's gotten in front of a truck. The big cab of a semi that's on its side. He backs the car up against it.

Tucked in here. Against the wall and semi.

He turns to look into the backseat. Headlights from the vehicles around them shine at angles through their car. The kids stare at their father.

"We're fine," he says. Reaching back. Holding their hands. Touching their knees. He'd like to get back there with them. But he knows he shouldn't. He'd like to curl up with them both, hold them, anything to protect them. But he shouldn't. He should sit. Right where he is. And wait for the crashing to stop.

• • •

In the Gulf, one oil rig is gotten under control. Hundreds of people working day and night finally stop the fire. It took them nearly two weeks. But they've stopped the oil leak. The well is sealed.

On barges out in the Gulf, under stars and a moon so bright it's like they could light the whole world on their own, the workers stand and cheer.

The abuse starts in foster care. From a foster parent. Before the woman can get her boy back. She's allowed only visitations. Until she proves herself to be fit and able. Proves she has a place to live that is of an adequate, appropriate standard.

The abuse starts. She can see it. In her boy. How he changes. Quiet. He won't talk.

During a visit, the woman simply takes her boy and leaves. Running with her son. A backpack for him. Another for herself. They run. Across the overpass. The only place that she can think to go. They'll hide there. Flee. To the city that's been abandoned.

CHAPTER 20

LADDERS

Thousands of people emerge from their cars.

Slowly.

It rains still, but some light has returned. The normal gray. The constant dim.

To the south, the storm still grinds above the South End.

But in the highway trench, no one can see what's happening.

Instead people just stand next to their cars. Looking around.

The quiet is real. It's not just a reflection of the blankness in their minds. The highway is quiet. For the first time, surely, since it was long ago constructed.

No cars drive. Few engines run.

People continue to emerge from their cars. Standing. Looking numbly and emptily around.

• • •

In the SUV, the woman stares at the others. Dead faces. Five of them.

Driver. Three analysts.

The boy.

• • •

The restaurant manager stands. Next to his car. It's untouched. And he is fine.

But around him, every car is wrecked in some way. Rear-ended. Dented. Turned sideways. Turned completely over.

He begins to realize there is a sound nearby. A muffled sound.

People. In their vehicles. All around him. He hears them as they wail.

• • •

His kids stare at him. In the mirror.

He stares back.

It isn't real.

This isn't real.

"Daddy," his daughter now says quietly. With a broken, final desperation. "Daddy, where is Mom?"

• • •

He stands at the rail, looking down at the cars and trucks and people on the highway. The kid, a former carousel operator, is a mile or more from any on-ramp leading down into that trench. But there's an overpass. A block away. He starts walking there. He doesn't know why.

In no sense does he know what he should do.

Mostly he wonders when someone will come to help those people.

• • •

Her husband bleeds. From his head.

And he won't wake. She's tried. Even though he breathes, he won't wake.

Her son still lies on the floor of the backseat. Eyes open. Staring up. Toward the top of the car. Her son now looks at his mother. Staring.

Her son says, "It's hard to explain what's happened."

The mother just barely smiles. Looking down at him. "I know, sweetie," she says. "I know."

• • •

The doctor and his wife walk out onto the steps of the cathedral. A light rain falls. The streets seem messy in a way they weren't before. Dirt. And shingles. Unidentifiable debris.

But otherwise, the North End looks the same.

They see people walking. Some quickly. All headed somewhere. South.

His wife asks a woman where they're going.

"The highway," she says. Next to her stands a young boy. He looks up at the wife. Then looks at the doctor. The doctor smiles at him.

But the boy still only stares. Takes his mother's hand. And continues to lead her toward the highway.

• • •

People gather on the one overpass crossing the trench. People from the North End. Residents. There are ten of them. Later there are twenty. Looking over the rail. One even sits on the railing of the overpass, bare feet dangling above the highway.

Below, on the surface of the highway, people have mostly gotten back into their vehicles. It's raining. Cold.

Everyone waits for help to come.

They've waited for a few hours.

The trail of stopped and damaged vehicles goes miles in each direction. Not that all are wrecked. But all of them are stuck now. In the shoulders of the highway or along the narrow median, or they are stuck in the middle lanes jammed in between so many other cars. There's no way anyone can drive. Not until many, many vehicles are somehow pushed aside.

Hours pass.

On car radios people hear of the massive destruction the storm has caused in the South End. The storm sped over the North End and the highway, touching it lightly by comparison to what it would then do in the South End. There, the storm slowed, lowered, let loose multiple tornadoes. No one

220

has a firm count. A wind insane, a weight those million people felt, every one of them, the storm held a weight each person knows now and will not ever forget.

In the South End, there is chaos.

Power out. Fires. Flooding. Looting of stores and office buildings. An unleashing of pent-up anger. Anger at the way things have always been. The unfairness of this city. Poor districts, rich ones. White districts, brown. Anger among those who were relegated to the flood zones. Isolated there since the moment this place was formed. Now flooded disproportionately. Their homes, their schools, their businesses bore the brunt of it. Anger now expressed through destruction, the tearing down of anything that withstood the storm. Anything that represents the unfairness inherent here.

News reports are intermittent. The TV and radio stations lost power too. Satellites disabled. Antennae knocked down. Fiber connections completely severed.

A city in chaos. With no plan for how to respond.

$$\cdots$$

She stays in the car with the dead people who once worked for her. Until finally she realizes she doesn't want to be here. The car is on its side. Dead people all around her. One leg touches her arm.

She doesn't want to be here.

The woman climbs over the boy, dead, his face so still and hard, and she barely recognizes it.

She escapes out the broken windshield. Now standing on the highway. Looking around at the others standing here too.

She'd been in the SUV for many hours. Some of the time, she closed her eyes. She may have slept. Waking and then looking carefully at each face. But mostly, she stared forward. Replaying each moment of the wreck. The SUV hit something. Flipped. In the car, people began to hit each other. Slamming against the ceiling. Seats. Against each other once again. Then other cars hit them. Three or four or five of them. She had soon lost count.

Now, standing on the highway, she's still not right. She knows that much.

She turns, turns again. The on-ramp they'd used to get onto this highway is a few miles back.

She decides to walk.

What she needs is help.

. . .

The restaurant manager sits in his car. Rain falls on his window. Lightly. The wipers periodically wash it away.

He sits. He's slept unintentionally. Many more hours pass.

Around him, people have gotten back into their cars. Ahead of him, he sees people gathered on the overpass.

The wailing stopped eventually. From the people in cars around him. They're all silent now. He doesn't know how many found a way to contain their pain. Or how many simply wailed until they died.

The radio broadcasts are intermittent. But he knows the storm did major damage in the South End. And so he wonders about his brother. His cell phone won't work. He checks often. Still no signal.

Although he's not sure his brother would even think to update him.

A woman is walking past his car. Pausing every three or four steps. Hesitating.

He rolls down his window. She's paused again. Right next to his car.

"Are you okay?" he asks.

It's a moment, then she turns to him. Some part of him realizes that she's beautiful. It's fact, not attraction. He's not of a mind to be attracted. It's simply that she's so very beautiful.

She's looking at him. "I can't remember," she says. "I can't remember which way I was meaning to walk."

"Do you want to sit?" he says. "Just sit. For a minute."

She stares at him. In another moment, he sees her nod. She opens the back door of his car. And soon she sits down in silence.

222

• • •

He climbs into the backseat with his kids. As he did what seems like months ago. On that hill overlooking the delta.

"Your mother," he says, holding both their hands. Looking at them. "Sweeties. Mom died."

• • •

He stands at the far end of the overpass. Looking down at the destruction. It's been hours now. A few people have left their cars. Started walking. But no one has come to help.

For a time he sits. The rain is not heavy, just enough to make his face wet. His hands wet.

He does not know where he will go.

He could stay here, right here on this overpass, and no one would ever care. Not one other person. All these millions of people, he's realized, as he's traveled across the country. All of them have their own lives.

He understands none of them. He likes none of them. He is a friend to no one, anywhere, at all.

• • •

She gets out of the car. Her son sleeps. Her husband will not wake. The bleeding's stopped. And he breathes. But he won't wake up.

She looks around. *Why doesn't anyone come to help?*

A few other people stand. Here on the highway. It's been hours now. Overnight. No one has come. Nothing.

She wonders if they should begin to walk.

She looks up at the sky. Rain touches her face. Rain that's harder now. Steady.

What do I do?

From the car, her son says, "Mom, are you okay?"

And she smiles. She has to. Despite it all. There's her son.

"Mom, come back to the car."

She's about to get in. Still looking down. Still smiling.

But she realizes that her toes are wet. Her shoes are submerged.

She sees it. All across the highway.

The water is already a few inches deep.

• • •

The doctor and his wife stand on the overpass. Thirty people here. All seem to be from the North End. They see the man who'd been sweeping church steps. The minister, people call him. He sits on the rail, bare feet dangling above the highway.

The minister and others talk. The doctor can't hear them. But suddenly the small group is worried. As if something is about to happen. Something imminent. Danger.

The doctor, without meaning to, turns, looks over his shoulder, up into the sky. Fearing there's another storm.

There isn't.

One of the men in the group has stepped away. The doctor's wife taps the man's arm. Asks him, "What is happening?"

The man looks at her. It seems to take a moment for him to understand the question. Repeating it to himself. He holds a camera. He looks down at it. Shifts it from one hand to the other. Looks up at the doctor. Then the wife. In another moment, the man says, "The highway. All this area. But especially the highway. It was built below sea level."

The doctor looks down to the highway. Water is pooling everywhere. A few inches of it.

"That's not rain?" the doctor asks.

The man with the camera looks up at the sky. Seeming to consider the question. He turns to the doctor. Stares a moment. "No," he says finally. "I thought you'd heard. The highway's flooding."

Then the man raises his camera. And takes a picture of them both.

• • •

The storm did not kill anyone in the North End.

But it did hit a levee. Breaching it. A levee near the highway. Which leaks now. More and more. Water that soon is slowly rising from the sewers underneath the highway. Near the overpass, the people on the highway have only just begun to notice the water pooling beneath all the cars and trucks and people.

And in some places, in lower points in that trench, especially near the on-ramps, the water there is already a few feet deep.

• • •

Everyone on the highway has begun to realize the water is rising.

The woman, the investor, sitting now in the backseat of this stranger's car, looks out the window and, even in her numbed and distant state, knows that this is not just rain.

"Something's wrong," she says.

Six inches. Here next to the overpass.

The man in front of her turns in his seat. Looks at her.

"The water," she says. "That's not just rain."

People are walking this way. From the east and west. She rolls down her window. "Why are you coming this way?" she asks.

A man answers her without stopping. "Because back there," he says, voice fading as he keeps walking, "the water there is even deeper."

• • •

The restaurant manager looks at the woman. Once again, she leans her head out the window. Looking down.

He opens his door. Looking down too. Water. Deep. It almost reaches the bottom of the car.

"We need to go," he says.

225

She looks around. He does too. The walls of the highway. No on-ramp, no exit, for miles either way.

She asks him in a minute, "Where?"

He shakes his head. Says, "I don't know." He's opening the door. "But we have to go."

And still, these many hours later, no one has come to help.

• • •

When he sees a massive ladder drop down from the overpass, the father thinks he's reached a point of perpetual madness. Shared unintentionally with his children. Holding them as they cry. All three of them curled up together in the backseat of the car.

The water has been rising.

He's been trying to come up with a plan.

Realizing, once again, that the three of them are on their own.

"Okay," he says quietly. "Okay. I'm sorry. But you have to listen now. We have to go. We have to get out of here."

He opens the door to the car. Water laps against the bottom of the door frame. He looks over to the ladder that's been dropped from the overpass to the surface of the road.

"Okay," he says softly. "Come on. We're leaving."

The children cry.

"I know," their father says. "I know."

He holds them once again. Looking over at that ladder.

"It's time," he whispers. "Come on. Because now we're going to climb."

• • •

Men and women in trucks come from what people call the North End. Bringing ladders. The former carousel operator watches this. A huge metal ladder is lowered to the surface of the highway. Soon more ladders follow. Some are clearly taken from fire stations; others are three sections long, used by painters and repairmen to climb to the roofs of tall houses and tall buildings. Still other people are beginning to lash smaller ladders together. The people have rope and wire and soon they begin to carefully slide the ladders over the rail along the overpass, lowering them to the people below.

He has seen a lot of things. This is one of the strangest.

The former carousel operator moves closer to the people working.

A woman turns to him. She's scarred deeply across her throat. On her wrists, there are bracelets. Twenty or thirty of them. He sees they are made of simple objects. Electrical wire. A thin strip of aluminum, brightly painted, torn carefully from a drink can. Leather strings tied with knots. A lace of sorts, wrapped round and round her forearm.

She says, in a moment, "Help us."

But he can only stare.

• • •

The water rises. It's above her knees. Her son sits on the hood of the car. Staring around.

The woman tries again to wake her husband. He sits in the passenger seat. Water in the car. Up to his waist now.

"Please," she says to her husband. "Come on. Please. Wake up."

She decides to pull him out. Awkwardly. Jerking his body some as she struggles to move him. She worries she is only hurting him more. But she can't leave him in this water for much longer.

People move to the west, wading through the water, others hopping from the top of one vehicle to another. Near her, people are beginning to exit a bus, their bodies sinking into the slowly moving water, their legs and waists now covered.

She's able finally to get her husband from his seat. He floats mostly, as she holds his head above the water. Still unconscious.

Her son sits on the hood of the car.

"We have to go," the mother says.

Her son slides off the hood. Water up to his thighs. He's tiny. Just a skeleton. There is so little left of him. "Let me get dad's arm," he says.

And so they leave, following the group west, as they pull her husband, his father, the man whose legs float limply in the rising water.

. . .

More ladders come. More rope.

How could these people have all these things?

His wife is about to help the people unload the trucks. Anything. She will help.

The doctor kisses her.

"People are hurt," she says. "Help them."

He looks down at the surface of the highway.

So far, only four of the ladders are long enough to reach the people below. The other ladders are still being combined. Tied together safely.

But the four ladders that reach the surface, no one has yet started to climb them.

. . .

The people who scavenge the North End are themselves a kind of community. They live together. Work together. Work that changes them.

Or maybe they are people who wanted to be changed. Who wanted the purpose of brutal work and a shared community.

Hundreds of them.

When they saw what was happening on the highway, it was clear to all of them what they would do.

Ladders. As many ladders as they could find or make.

. . .

The woman, once an investor, follows the man she's met. She doesn't know his name. She forgot to ask. But now they move through water above their waists. Sometimes they can get on top of vehicles, hop from one car to the next. Mostly, though, they slosh through the cold and fetid water, moving with a growing crowd.

She is about to jump from the roof of a car to a truck next to it. The man she's with has stopped. He points to the space between the vehicles.

Cattle pass. Released or broken free of a transport trailer. They move between the cars and trucks. Walking west.

She can only stare.

• • •

Behind him, he sees chickens. On the tops of cars. There are pigs now, among the cattle. Swimming. The water's too deep for them to walk.

Rain still falls. On his face.

The woman next to him points toward the west.

He looks as, in a moment, she says, "Ladders."

• • •

Still no one has climbed. The father and his children reach the base of the first ladder. The man touches the rung in front of him. The ladder shakes. He looks up to the top. Sixty feet. A terrifying climb.

"Daddy," his son says. "I can't do that."

His daughter stares up too.

"Yes," the father says. "You can. You will. We all three will."

The father climbs as close as he can to his children. But still they are alone. Above him. Both screaming for him to help. The first ones, he has realized. They are the first ones to climb these ladders.

• • •

He stands watching these people assembling the ladders. Tying ropes to them. Safety lines.

But the former carousel operator can't find a way to help.

They near the overpass, still pulling her husband through the water. Soaked, mother and son and father; the rain falls steadily, and there's a current to the water now. Chickens float past them. Some are flapping wildly, most have already died.

There are bodies too. Of so many other people.

They float inside their cars.

• • •

The doctor goes to the minister, the man from the steps of the church. "I can help," he says. "I'm a doctor."

The minister smiles. Lightly grabs both of the doctor's shoulders. "Wonderful."

It's minutes later that the doctor realizes the minister spoke to him in Spanish.

Scavengers have already begun to set up tents. Huge tents. Military. From an abandoned depot here. The minister takes the doctor into one of them. "There are injured people," the minister says. "Tell us what to do."

On the overpass, his wife works on the ropes. Tying them together. Attaching ropes every ten feet along the surface of the ladders.

Safety lines. One after another. She ties as quickly as she can.

• • •

Still no one has come from the South End to help. No ambulances. No firefighters. No police. No one.

Word reaches the overpass that the chaos in the South End has only begun to grow.

• • •

The woman stands in the ad hoc line. Moving toward the base of one of the ladders. The man is still with her. She keeps meaning to ask his name.

She looks at him now. He's turned to her. "Thank you," she says.

He nods. "Yes," he says. "Of course."

In another moment, she begins to climb.

• • •

He makes sure she gets started on the ladder. Upward. Just two or three people can get on a ladder at one time. So he sees her rising. She's midway up before he also starts.

The ladder bounces and shakes as he climbs too now, the bouncing soon seeming uncontrollable. He hates heights. But the horror that he sees as he gets higher, the horror of the hours spent on this abandoned highway, all that numbs his fear of being thirty feet, now forty feet up; each step he is higher up in the air.

Destroyed cars. A gathering of hundreds of people. More making their way to these ladders. Dead people, bodies, everywhere.

Some part of him thinks he should cry. Because his mother died. Because he lives alone. Because he barely knows his brother. Because his life is not what he wants.

All reasons he should cry.

But the man just climbs.

The woman has reached the top. People help her over the rail.

Some part of him wonders if she'll be there when he gets to the top.

• • •

"Keep climbing," the father says, repeating himself, speaking to his children. "Slowly. Don't worry. One foot. One hand. One foot. One hand."

Which they do. Again and again. Even as they scream. Above him. Alone. The only sound is their screaming.

• • •

The former carousel operator watches people reach the railing of the over-pass. Climbing up from below. People up here help them. They help them over the rail, and they help them get to one of the tents that've been set up, and there are people now bringing food and water.

He stands. People moving all around him. But still he can only stand. Watching the others help.

· · ·

She and her son place the body on the roof of a pickup truck. Tall enough, she hopes, that the water won't wash him away.

Although that doesn't really matter.

Somewhere, during the walk, he stopped breathing.

Her son cries.

She does too.

We have to climb, she thinks.

But for now, she'll just stand with her son and cry.

· · ·

The doctor goes from person to person. There are broken bones. Gashes across arms and faces.

But mostly there is confusion. Desperation. Shock.

How could that have happened?

His wife ties ropes. Attaches them to ladders. Helps as they are lowered to the surface.

He sees her, on the other end of the overpass. Working. For a moment, he has stepped outside the tent. Washing his hands and face. Breathing and closing his eyes. Drinking water from a mug, water so cold and it's bright almost, different than anything he's ever tasted.

He drinks from it again.

He feels like he should drink this for the rest of his whole life.

A wall of people, it seems, all climbing up from the highway. Attackers assaulting a castle. Or the nearly drowned now rescued from the ocean, steadily scaling the side of a ship.

On the surface of the highway, hundreds more still wait. Standing on cars and trucks. Shuffling in place. Looking up at the people climbing. Looking down at the water rising.

• • •

She sits under a blanket. On this overpass. People all around her. Sitting or lying down. Some walk; she sees others run when they get to the surface of this overpass; she sees some of them look around, afraid, and they run.

She can't imagine what they fear up here, the former investor. Her fear was left on the highway. It poured from her as she climbed.

She hadn't been afraid in many years. Since she was a child. But as she climbed, she remembered fear.

She drinks some sort of coffee. Looks around.

Who are all these people?

She assumes she could walk south. To her hotel. Shower. Fly out. Or just drive away. Return to her silent office overlooking the city.

All she has to do is stand. And walk.

Other analysts and employees can be hired. Not what she wants. But it is true.

She drinks once more from the coffee. A woman near her, covered in jewelry made of wire and glass, helps lower another ladder over the side.

She drinks again from her coffee.

The man who helped her is gone. She wants to thank him. Wants to know his name. Thinks that he should know her name too.

• • •

The restaurant manager looks to the north. To the city that's been abandoned. The North End. He grew up in the south. Grew up fearing the North End. Grew up being told it was dangerous and blighted and that what happened there was deserved.

He pictures video of a house on fire, a man who lived there pulling his wife and children from the embers. Dead. That, he was told, was the North End.

Now, though, he sees that people keep coming from the North End to this overpass. Bringing food. Bringing blankets. A group of scarred and weathered people ride in the back of an old pickup truck, passing him; one raises her hand. Inside the truck, there are more tarps and rope and tents.

This is not what he knew of the North End.

He wonders where that woman went. Hoping that she is fine.

• • •

They sit underneath a blanket on the overpass. The three of them. His children lean into his sides.

The kids have eaten bread and soup. Handed to them by a woman; a man handed them the blanket.

He takes a drink of water. Then another. Gives his children some. "Drink more."

It is not enough to survive.

He pulls his children close. They smile some.

They lean into his sides.

They will do more than just survive.

• • •

He walks. Along the highway. Behind him, he can hear all those people gathered on that overpass, helping the ones who keep climbing up from the highway. He walks faster, his backpack bounces against his arms.

234

Ahead of him, he hears the chaos. Sirens in the South End. There are people screaming. But beyond that, there are other places.

Why? he tries to remember. *Why did I leave my three friends behind?*

What, he wonders, *is the girl maybe doing now?*

He smells smoke, and even in the night there are black plumes rising from neighborhoods around him, and above his head as he walks and thinks about the girl and his three friends, he can see the glow of fire in the clouds.

• • •

On the overpass, the son lets his mother hold him.

More loss than they can comprehend. More horrors than they can speak aloud. More sadness than they will ever want to think about or remember.

But the son lets his mother hold him.

Soaked and cold, and a woman gives them blankets as a young boy hands them some sort of drink. It steams.

They thank the woman. Thank the boy.

She holds her son. There's so little left. His thinness embodies all that's wrong. The mother feels every single bone.

Memories, childhood, games in the yard, her husband playing hide-and-seek, a father who always threw a ball, to this son and to his older brother.

"I wish everything had been different," the mother says. "I'm sorry about all that's happened. I am just so sorry."

And still the son lets his mother hold him.

• • •

The doctor has been moving throughout the tents. Helping people with their injuries.

"No one comes to help," his wife says. They stand together for a minute.

He shakes his head.

"How is that possible?" she asks.

He shakes his head again.

"We're supposed to fear that place," she says, nodding toward the North End.

"Do you?" he asks her.

"No," she says.

He leans close to her. He can smell her hair.

She kisses him.

"There are people to help," she says.

He kisses her. "Yes," he says. "Please you go and help them."

· · ·

On the highway, what's left behind are the carcasses. Of the livestock released or broken free. And of the people who could not escape.

What caused this is not easily determined. Beyond the storm. The wrecks. The broken levee. And the horror.

On the highway are vehicles and refuse, and there is so much water, from the sky and from the sewers and from the bay to the north.

Around them is a fractured city, two cities now, separated by a highway, one gone and one in descent, and no one here is able to see either for what they are.

On the overpass, so many people, lost and broken and helped, each one now staggered, whether fleeing from a North End they've been told to fear or sitting in silence among so many other refugees from the storm or veering slowly toward that ruined city to the north, drawn to it; it's impossible, but that empty place does draw them forward.

But what caused this? This chaos, this abandonment, this destruction of people and place. Isn't there an answer? Shouldn't there be one? How can there not be a simple way of making sense of the insane?

Her boy lives.

But he's not the same.

He is silent now. Often, he just stares.

He wants with all his being to protect his mother.

At night, he reads. Quietly. She finds books for him in the abandoned library.

There's something he knows that she can't change. Can't eliminate.

She can only hold him tight.

EPILOGUE

A baseball game now ends. Somewhere. It ends soon after it begins. The weather. Wind. A storm too violent.

All of you, please go home.

• • •

He wonders about his children. The two of them. Held close.

Sorrow he can't comprehend. Does not experience. They are on their own.

He wants that to not be true. But there's nothing he can do to change it.

Your mother died.

Mom is dead.

Sweeties, she's no longer with us.

They don't cry now. They just sit. Here under these rough blankets. On an overpass. Near this city.

He won't stay here. They will leave. Find a place. A new home. With sunlight. Green trees. The hope of a life that is not so hard.

• • •

She stares at a group of people all equally scarred across their bodies. They repaired and replaced the ladders for hours as she sat here.

One has filaments of silver wrapped around her neck. Its creation must have involved a hundred passes. Round and round.

There are more of them. Thirty. They hardly talk. But they stand together.

She looks down at her clothes. A suit. She paid many thousands of dollars for it. Her shoes cost even more.

She stands too now. Walks over to the group of people. They don't speak. So quiet.

"Where is it," she asks them, "that all of you now live?"

. . .

The former restaurant manager helps load ropes and tools and gear into a pickup truck.

Someone nods to him.

He has nowhere to go. This is obvious. But still it is so sad.

Everyone fades away.

On the highway, in the crashing that he witnessed, he told himself his life would change. Become different. A life of substance.

He's aware that he's not alone. That hundreds and thousands on the highway likely also made a commitment of this type.

But he walks to the front of the pickup now. Taps on the driver's door. "What," he asks the man, "can I do to help?"

. . .

The former carousel operator finds a phone that works. In an office building. Nearby the sirens wail. They have not stopped in hours.

He's gone through many buildings. Here in the wreckage of the storm where it hit what's called the South End. Looking for a phone that works.

This one does. The building's lights are out. The front door and windows are broken. But the phone still works.

He doesn't know the girl's number. But he calls his dad.

"Tell me," his father says through the phone, tired, his dad has just woken up, "tell me all that you've chosen to do."

The kid listens. Thinks. But cannot respond.

He watched once as his father beat a man bloody in the parking lot of a fast-food restaurant. He watched once as his father coaxed a woman to leave her date in some dark and crappy bar. He watched once as his father threatened him, with consequences clear and violent, if he did not stand now and go to school.

"Has anyone ever called?" the kid asks his father.

There's silence. Then motion. His father moves, shifting on the couch or in his bed.

"There's one thing," he hears his father say. "Here it is. One thing. A number. From some girl."

• • •

Her son eats more food. As they sit together in this tent.

The mother drinks more water. It's no small thing. The water. It's as if she's been served a potion, or maybe it's a tonic?

"What do we do?" her son asks.

The mother holds him. Lightly. Arm across the bones of her son's thin back.

"He took us down a hole," her husband once said to her, speaking of their older child, as they sat on their front porch after their boy died; whether it was a fight or they cried or her husband talked to himself, she can't remember. "And at first it seemed like going down that hole with him would help. We would follow him and protect him. Save him. Make him better. But the farther down the hole we went, the more sick everyone in the house became. We weren't chasing him. He was pulling us, downward, closer and closer to the illness. And so our youngest son let go, he stopped along that descent. And then I was next. I let go. I stepped off of that dark and awful path. I feel a guilt about this that I will never overcome. But I did it. I let go. To save myself. And yet you didn't. You never let go. You held on to him. All the way down to the bottom of that hole he had created. Created unintentionally. But you stayed there with him. It's the greatest and best and most selfless thing you could ever do. But now you're stuck there. All alone."

She rubs her hand across her son's back.

She'll cry more. Later. Her husband died. She will cry more.

But now she holds her son. As best she can. Without breaking him. Sweet, sweet boy. He'll break if she holds him closer.

"We sit," the mother says, answering her son. Kisses him. Lightly. On the head. "We just sit."

• • •

The doctor holds his wife.

Although, as it's always been, it is she who holds her husband.

She whispers to him. Words that now soak into him. He absorbs each one.

For a moment, it's as if he's heard every sound she's ever made. Felt all of her movements. Smelled each scent that she now has.

He kisses her near the ear.

"Why?" she asks.

They sit together near the overpass. Soon, he'll return to help the wounded. Soon, she'll return to helping the many others still in need.

What she went through before he met her, he must now imagine. Not by choice. It's necessity. He must picture it. To love her is to understand.

"Why?" she asks again.

He has no answer. Or none that he will share.

And so he only kisses her.

• • •

They are the last to emerge from one of the vehicles on the highway. A bus, the front door opens. They swim through the filthy water, strewn with bodies, debris, and livestock. Ten girls, they swim to a ladder. Climb up to the overpass, one after another. No screaming, no noise; they clearly show no fear. Beautiful, each of them, girls maybe fifteen at most, in their dresses. Each dress white. Each dress the same. Soon they reach the overpass, gather together. The man who leads them looks around. At the others on the over-pass. At the girls who've climbed ahead of him.

He sees the faces of these strangers. Staring now at him.

In a moment, he nods. Then turns. Walks south. Away from here.

The girls look around the overpass. Then look at each other.

It's another few minutes before all begin to smile.

• • •

Out in the Gulf, a crew on a barge closes off another well. There's confirma-tion from the technician. It is announced on the loudspeakers above the deck.

The crew packs up its gear in silence, each person only looking down at the new work orders in their hands. They climb into boats that take them across the Gulf, the water thick with oil, coating the sides of the boat as it lurches heavily through thick waves, taking the crew to another rig, still bleeding; there are so many more that they must fix.

• • •

The minister sweeps the broad steps leading up to the cathedral. Turning again and again to welcome people from the overpass. People who come to pray.

He has always loved the church.

He simply had long periods when he would not let it love him back.

• • •

The woman sits near the tent. Watching her young son. Still he works. Going from person to person. Bringing blankets. Food and water. Whatever anyone wants or needs.

A kindness in him unbroken.

• • •

The man walks through the front doors of the hotel. He holds the camera in one hand. With the other he slowly pushes the hair out of his dim eyes.

Rainwater covers the floor.

He starts to walk toward the staircase that leads up to his room. Twenty floors above.

Today, though, he lets himself walk the long way across the lobby.

Much has happened. Since he sat here alone with her.

Normally, he doesn't walk this way. Under the atrium.

But today he does. After the storm.

Much has happened.

He pauses. Looks up. Floor after floor, metal railings; they rise up, seeming to bend slightly toward the top.

Once lit dimly.

Once a place he sat for hours.

Much has happened. Since he sat here alone with her. Since they later had a family, living together in this city.

Happiness. Darkness. All that seemed possible.

He sits alone. On the rotted sofa. Looking around. Looking up. Calculating.

All that was lost.

He sets his camera on a table. He pulls a small notebook from his pocket. Turns pages. Looks at the handwriting. Inky black. Letters forming words. A structure only he can follow. Words spilt out, one after another, across page after page after page.

• • •

The city dies. Like it has for years.

The city dies. And most just watch its collapse.

Cities die. These places that have gathered people in the millions.

How do they die? What happens? Why do so many people hate this place?

Your place.

Mine.

There is hatred.

There's abuse.

There are the decisions people make. To destroy and to neglect and to remove, removing people and attention and care.

Cities abandoned. Even those that are still inhabited. Cities can be abandoned.

Because there's a will to stay. Or to run away.

It's a choice.

So come now. Listen.

As the city cries your name.

ACKNOWLEDGMENTS

The author wishes to thank Elizabeth Trupin-Pulli for all of her support, as well as Cal Barksdale at Arcade Publishing. Thanks so much to you both. The author also wishes to thank all the writers who were kind enough to read and support *The City Where We Once Lived*. Much thanks also to all of the bartenders who tolerated that guy at the end of the bar with his head down, wearing earphones, taking up space for hours and hours and hours, especially everyone at the Beauty Shop, Sweet Grass Next Door, Second Line, and, for more hours than should ever be counted, Alchemy.

And, also, thanks to Nora. Always.